Asphalt Angels

Asphalt Angels

Ineke Holtwijk

Translated by Wanda Boeke

Front Street 8 Lemniscaat
Asheville, North Carolina

Copyright © 1995 by Lemniscaat b.v. Rotterdam
English translation copyright © 1999 by Wanda Boeke
Originally published in the Netherlands under the title *Engelen van het Asfalt*
Printed in the United States of America
Designed by Helen Robinson
All rights reserved
First Front Street paperback edition

Publication has been made possible with financial support from
THE FOUNDATION FOR THE
PRODUCTION AND TRANSLATION
OF DUTCH LITERATURE

Library of Congress Catalog-in-Publication Data
Holtwijk, Ineke.
[Engelen van het asfalt. English]
Asphalt Angels / Ineke Holtwijk; translated by Wanda Boeke.
p. cm.
Summary: Abandoned on the streets of Rio de Janeiro,
thirteen-year-old Alex joins a group of children like him
and finds himself adapting to his new life.
ISBN 1-886910-43-X (pb)
[1. Homeless persons – Fiction.
2. Rio de Janeiro (Brazil) – Fiction.
3. Brazil – Fiction] I. Boeke, Wanda.   II. Title.
PZ7.H7422As1998

[Fic] – dc21   98-13063

Contents

For all the Asphalt Angels,

those who dream

and those who don't dare dream anymore

Asphalt Angels

The Park

Would he be able to handle a night here? Alex looked at the concrete bench in the empty spot in the park. It was narrow. And hard. Maybe it was better to lie down in the grass under the tree. But what if there were animals? Stinging ants, maybe. Or spiders. Or a dog that started sniffing at him. The idea filled him with dread. No, better the hard bench.

The bench was very long and shaped like a horseshoe. Farther down a bum lay snoring. A little human heap in a flour sack, that was what he looked like. He probably walked around barefoot all the time. Shapeless black calloused hunks stuck out of the tattered pant legs. Alex shuddered.

Would he look like that too in a couple of weeks? If he were still alive. He looked down. There was nothing wrong with his plastic sandals—everybody had those. Boys who lived in houses, too. But they didn't have sand between their toes the way he did, because when they got home from the beach they took showers. The ocean had left salt stains on his black legs. Luckily he could get them off if he rubbed hard. Nobody would see the hole in his nylon shorts if he rolled them up. His T-shirt was clean—he had washed it yesterday in the river. No, Alex thought he actually looked pretty good. Nobody could tell that he had been thrown out of his house and was living on the street.

The bum didn't move. Maybe he was dead. The thought terrified Alex. "Ghhruk," said the corpse and the burlap bag rolled over. "Thank God," mumbled Alex. Another dead person, that would be the last straw.

From the bench he could see the beach through the trees and even the little lights on the other side of the bay. The hills were dark, plump shadows. Like a herd of sleeping cows. It must be at least eleven o'clock, Alex figured, but people were still walking up and down the asphalt path along the beach. Bright floodlights lit up the white sand almost all the way to the bay.

The volleyball players gave the ball dull slaps. On the low stone wall dividing the path from the park sat drummers in their swimsuits. One of them was drumming along with a stick on a can. They were singing a samba:

> Coconut tree where the coconuts grow,
> where I hang my hammock
> on clear moonlit nights—
> ah, Brazil
> for me,
> for me, it's Brazil.

Now and then the tinkling of a bicycle bell or shouts would ring out.

Alex spread out the newspaper he'd found near the trash can. He folded over the top of his plastic bag of clothes so that he could use it as a pillow, and he lay down. His feet hurt from walking. If it were possible, he'd unscrew them.

He closed his eyes, but he didn't like the feeling at all. His heart seemed to be pounding even harder. That was strange.

There was a rustling noise behind him. What was that? He pricked up his ears. It rustled again. Could it be somebody walking? He turned his head carefully and looked. The stretch of grass under the trees was empty, but the tree trunks were so big that somebody could easily be standing behind them. Some twigs snapped. Alex was breathing heavily and his mouth was dry. What should he do? Run away? He opened his eyes wide, but nothing happened. He got hold of himself. It must have been a rat.

Nothing happened for so long that his eyes slowly closed again. That wasn't good. He had to stay awake. At least one eye open, so that he could see danger approaching. He rolled onto his back and stared at the sky. He saw no stars or clouds. He saw only images. Like a video clip, the day ran through his head.

He saw himself walking down the dirt path by the dump on the way home. There were his former school friends. "Hey, Alex. How you doing? Too bad about your mom."

"What? What about my mom?"

"She's dead. Didn't you know?"

He ran home. There was the Volkswagen van that was used for funerals. He felt hot and then ice cold. It couldn't be true. She was still so young. The little board over the ditch thumped as he ran inside.

The room was crowded. He saw neighbors, his older brother Pito and his wife, and "the guy," which was what he called his stepfather, and the guy's daughters. A neighbor lady was sobbing in great bursts. "No, no. My God, no. She can't die!" He pushed his way between the bodies. On the spot where the couch normally stood, his mother lay in a casket on trestles. She had her eyes closed as if she were sleeping. Her face was as white as the dishes in the kitchen. Her hair was longer than when he had last seen her, three months earlier, before she went to the hospital. It seemed as if she might wake up any minute, but he knew she wouldn't. He was looking at an empty body. The only person he had in the whole world had flown away. She would never again hug him to her. She would never again run her fingers through his hair. The move, the course he was going to take ... All the plans, shattered. She had handed him over to that guy.

"She didn't want to put up with it anymore. She pulled the tubes out," his brother's wife whispered to a neighbor lady.

"What do you expect ... Three months on an IV and no future."

He whirled around.

"Where you going?" his brother called out.

He didn't answer but ran to the little soccer field at the end of the path.

That was where he'd sat down. He'd seen how the funeral party had filed toward the cemetery. After about an hour he had gone back. Only Bruno, his younger brother, was home. Bruno had cried when he saw Alex collecting his clothes. He had given Bruno his baseball cap and soccer ball. "Don't cry, Bruno. Someday I'll be back. Then I'll be rich and I'll come take you out of this place," he had said.

Then they'd heard the thump of the board. He estimated his chances. Would he be able to get away through the hole in the wall and across the yard without being noticed? Too late. There stood his stepfather, big and booming. "How dare you show your face here, you good-for-nothing punk! You, nothing but lies all the time. You didn't get the message, did you? You're not welcome here anymore!"

Alex felt his head grow hot and light. Before he could think, he blurted out, "Now you got what you want. You can smoke in the bedroom. Drink beer. Don't need to take your whores in the bushes anymore. You can have all forty other members of your family over. You can—"

He couldn't finish his sentence. He hit the wall with his stepfather's arm resting heavily on his chest. The pockmarked face hung right above him and yelled, "I'll kill you like a dog if you ever dare set foot in this house. A bullet is what you got coming. Now beat it, freeloader!"

A spray of spittle settled on his face, but Alex couldn't wipe it off because he was pinned. He felt sick to his stomach from the sour beer smell that wouldn't go away.

When his stepfather finally let him go, he had grabbed the plastic bags and left without a word. He wouldn't have been able to say anything even if he had wanted to. His throat was swollen and dry as if it were full of foam rubber.

He had left his clothes and his sneakers with his buddy Sergio. "If you haven't heard from me in a couple of months, it means I'm dead. Then you can have them," he had said. Sergio had said nothing. Alex had taken along only an extra pair of shorts and two T-shirts in a plastic bag. Sergio's mother had given him a package of coconut cookies for the road. Then he'd taken the train to the city—the train known as the "stock car" because it's so crowded and stinks of sweat and urine.

Feeling numb, he had walked around the streets lined with skyscrapers. He didn't really know what to do. Where could he go? Then he remembered the park. His mother used to have a cleaning job somewhere around there. He had gone along a couple of times and remembered having seen street kids with blankets in the park.

He found it easily. It was located close to downtown in the curve of the bay. First there was the beach, and around it, like a giant comma, lay the park. He had walked on asphalt paths and little bridges. He had climbed up hills and looked around the soccer fields. Nowhere had he seen street kids. Not on the beach, either. He hadn't wanted to ask anybody. What if they thought he was a street kid?

The thought startled Alex. Maybe he was a street kid. He had slept on the street before sometimes, but now it was different. He didn't have a house anymore. Or a mother. He had nothing anymore.

Wham! There was the casket with the white face popping into his head again. He didn't want to think about it, but the videotape kept running on its own. Where was her spirit wandering now? Was she in heaven? Was it nighttime there too? Maybe spirits never slept. Alex stared at the sky. Big gray clouds floated by. He decided that his mother was awake and was looking down at him from the sky. The idea reassured him. As if she were watching over him just a little bit. Suddenly it wasn't quite so scary to go to sleep.

Robson

A train with a thundering roar was heading straight for Alex. He was lying on the tracks, and no matter how he tried to get up, it didn't work. He could hear the engine wail and a whistle blow. Then he woke up. On the airstrip out in the bay an airplane had landed. The engines shrieked.

The sun was shining, but it still wasn't very hot out. That fig-ured—it was winter. On the grass stood a small group of people. Most of them were women, and they flapped their arms at a young man's signals. Cyclists in cycling outfits whizzed by on the asphalt path. At the end of the concrete bench sat an old man in shorts reading the paper. The bum lay in his rags a little far-ther down, as if he hadn't moved an inch the whole night. Nobody seemed to be paying any attention to him.

Alex was thirsty and hungry. Suddenly he remembered the

cookies. He fished the pieces out from among his clothes in the plastic bag. Dumb, he thought. He had slept on them. Now he had to find water. Where had he seen the tap where people filled their thermoses?

Near the beach Alex found the tap. He drank, washed his face, rinsed his sandy feet and his legs. And when nobody was looking, he pulled the elastic waistband of his shorts out as if he were nine months pregnant and let the stream run down his belly and into his shorts.

He wasn't wearing underwear; he hadn't ever had any. Quickly he slipped his hand between his legs and slapped water over his crotch. He rubbed an imaginary piece of soap over his stomach. Done. Clean.

"Good lord, has this turned into some kind of public shower?"

He jumped and turned around. Behind him stood an old woman with a sunhat on and a poodle. The blood drained out of his cheeks. He didn't know how to act. Had she seen anything?

She laughed. "If you ask me, you're a little wet behind the ears."

He clutched at his ears. Only then did he realize that she was making a joke.

She ignored him after that. "Come on, Pretinha, your turn," she said to the poodle. She pulled at the leash. "We're going to have a nice little turn under the tap."

She obviously didn't have children, thought Alex.

On a stone wall he let himself dry off in the sun. A huge oil tanker was making its way through the bay. Now and then an airplane would skim over the water. In order to reach the landing strip the planes had to drop so low that their bellies almost touched the surface.

"Watch it, watch out." A man was pedaling up the path. Hitched to the bicycle was a wobbly metal cart with thin logs of ice at least three feet long in it.

He'd better be quick, thought Alex. The ice logs were melting as he watched. There was a long trail of water drops on the path. The man kicked out the stand and tossed a rag over his shoulder, then ran up the beach with a log of ice. "Watch it, watch out." The ice log was delivered at a beach bar and beaten to bits for the coolers. By the time he got to the second ice log, his bicycle was parked in the middle of a puddle.

The beach started filling up with sunbathers. They came from all directions with folding chairs and beach umbrellas under their arms. There were lots of mothers with children, groups of friends. He saw hardly anybody going by themselves. Some were hauling radios and coolers of food.

Alex smelled fried onions. Farther down a hot dog cart had stopped. In a frying pan as big as a tire the hot dog man was frying onions and tomatoes.

Alex had never paid attention to it before, but the beach was crowded although it was the middle of the week. Didn't these people have to go to work? He thought of Bruno, who had slept by himself in the twin bed and was now at school. Just like Sergio.

I can do as I please, thought Alex. But without any money, what was the point?

What did a street kid do during the day, anyway? He could think of nothing but swimming or playing soccer. If they sold candy, where did they put the candy at night? If they polished shoes, they had a wooden chest that had to go somewhere. Or would they hide that in the bushes?

"Hey, weren't you lying on the bench?"

A boy had come and sat down beside him. He was almost a head shorter than Alex and not as black. His skin was the color of toffee, and his hair wasn't kinky like Alex's but thick and wavy.

"Look, that's where I was," he said without waiting for an answer. "See that white thing on the other side of the trees?"

Alex leaned forward and saw a building that looked mostly like a concrete merry-go-round without any animals on it.

"That's a band shell."

"Hmm," said Alex. He didn't know what a band shell was, but he wasn't going to let on to this boy.

"I work for Dona Lica in the bar."

"Oh," said Alex.

"There, on the beach. I just chipped the ice." The boy showed his wet arms. The sharp edges of the ice had cut his arms. He was even bleeding. He pulled a can of Coke out of his shorts pocket. "Earned it. You want some?" The boy smiled. He had nice white teeth, not little black stumps like Alex's.

"Hmm," Alex said again, hesitating. He did want some.

The boy shoved the can into his hands. "Don't give me that, man."

They sat there a while and watched the joggers passing by and the girls in bikinis.

"My name's Robson," the boy said after a long silence. "What's yours?"

"Alex."

"How old are you?"

"Thirteen," said Alex.

"I'm fourteen," declared Robson. "Did you run away too?"

Alex nodded. "I'm from Japeri," he said. "You know where that is?"

Robson shook his head.

"That's two hours away by train unless it stops somewhere."

"Did they beat you?" Robson wanted to know.

Alex sat up. "If the guy ever started punching, I'd hit him back. No, that wasn't the problem. My mother died. And the guy, I mean my stepfather, is out to get me. He kicked me out of the house because he wants to have everything for himself."

Robson looked at him. "Damn, stepfathers suck. First they move in on your mother and then they tell you to get the hell out. What about your mother?"

"My mother always stood up for me. 'If he goes, I go,' she'd say. She was on my side. When she went into the hospital, he didn't let me eat at the house anymore. Now she's dead. There was something wrong with her intestines or something." Alex tried to talk fast so he didn't have to think. When he talked about his mother and her being dead, his heart grew heavy. As if there were a wet towel hanging over it. He looked at Robson out of the corner of his eye. The boy hadn't noticed a thing.

"My father's a *cachaçeiro*," said Robson. "Falls down drunk every day. Pounded all of us. Never had any money. It all got spent on *rum*. My mother's dead. But she never did anything to stop it. Every time he promised he'd quit, and she believed him. I broke out, though. I'm not crazy. No grub at home and then they go and get on your case too. I'd rather be on the street. You don't have any grub there either, but at least you can do what you feel like." Robson paused and glanced up. "I'd say it's almost noon."

Alex was blown away by how coolly Robson talked about home.

"Dona Lica," Robson shouted. When the woman with bleached-blond hair tending the bar looked up, he tapped his wrist with his index finger.

She understood immediately. "Twelve-thirty," she hollered back.

"Whoa, Alex, we better get moving." He waved at Dona Lica, who had collected beer-drinking men under her beach parasol, and jumped off the wall.

Alex followed. He had nothing better to do anyway. Besides, he was curious. What was this Robson up to?

They walked out of the park and into the neighborhood. Its name, like the park's, was Flamengo. The streets were narrow and lined with trees. There was a miniature castle with turrets and stairs on the corner. Behind it the housing complexes began, tall apartment buildings. Where rich people lived.

There was a big difference between rich people and poor people, Alex thought. In Flamengo there weren't any dirt paths or potholes in the street, as there were in Japeri. The walls were white and you never saw any windows covered with cardboard. Everybody had glass. When you went to visit somebody, you first had to go through a tall gate that was locked. After that there was usually a glass door that was also locked. Somewhere in the lobby there was a doorman behind a console. If he wanted to open the door, he pushed a button. Inside, everything was big and new. A wide hallway, mirrors, tiled floors, a swimming pool on the roof. That was how the building his mother had worked in had looked. That was how the apartment building to which Robson brought him that afternoon looked.

"This is where we're going to eat," said Robson as the glass door buzzed open, and he sprinted toward the elevator.

Robson's aunt lived in the apartment. No, not his real aunt. She was more like a kind of friend, Robson said. He knew her from the beach. She went to the beach a lot, usually with her daughter. She always looked around to see if Robson was there. One day she'd said, "Why don't you come eat lunch with us?" So Robson got a house where he could eat every day, take a shower, and change clothes. Because she kept his bag of clothes for him.

"Well now, is everything all right? You two are late," said the woman who opened the door. She had little curls and was on the heavy side. She acted as if it were normal that Robson had brought him along. "My name's Vera," she said, smiling, to Alex. She threw her arm around him and pulled his head to her chest.

"His name's Alex," said Robson.

Alex smelled flowers and something else. It made him dizzy. Rich people even smell different from poor people, he thought.

"Go take a shower, quick. Then we can eat," said Vera, letting him go.

Alex felt strange as he sat down at the table. As if he were walking around in a movie. The kitchen at home had a hard dirt floor and they cooked with bottled gas. Water had to be fetched. Here there were tiles, a shiny sink, and a big stove with six burners. And there was as much food as he wanted. Rice, beans, meat, salad.

Robson talked a blue streak. About the iceman, about Dona Lica, whom Vera also knew, and her bar, about some jogger who'd been robbed of his track shoes in the park, about the new fence around the utility shed. Vera smiled a lot, and now and then she winked at Alex.

Alex ate in silence and tried not to look at Vera's daughter. She was sitting straight across from him and kept staring at him. He tried to eat in such a way that she wouldn't see his teeth. He was ashamed of the cemetery of black stumps in his mouth, and he desperately hoped nobody had noticed the rip in his shorts. A fancy house like this ... Too bad he couldn't tell Bruno.

Then he had to go to the bathroom.

"Marlene, will you show Alex where the bathroom is?" asked Vera. The girl who had stared at him the whole time got up.

"Here's the light switch," she said as she opened a door.

Alex stepped in. He didn't lock the door. What if he couldn't get it unlocked again? He sat down comfortably. Who knew how long it would be before he sat on a real toilet again? There were mirrors, mats, and little bottles everywhere. The tiles had flowers on them. This Vera must be really rich.

When he was done, he wanted to flush, but he couldn't find the rope to pull. There wasn't a bucket, either. He was starting to sweat. He peered at the ceiling. Nothing. There was a cup on the vanity. He filled it and emptied it into the bowl. Then another one, and another quickly after that. Nothing happened. "C'mon, go down," he pleaded. He tried being stern: "Yo, beat it. Go on down." But the giant turd lay motionless.

If he went to get Robson, the girl was sure to come too, to see what was the matter. Alex started sweating even more at the idea. Cover it! Quick, toilet paper, and then get Robson.

"Jesus, man, what have you been doing?" asked Robson when he came into the bathroom and saw all the loops of toilet paper spilling out from under the toilet seat cover. "Carnival's over, you know. Man, it stinks in here."

"Robson, please, shhhh." Alex thumped his back to get him to shut his mouth. "Help me. I don't know how you're supposed to flush. Where's the rope?"

Robson leaned over and pushed a brass box on the wall. The waterfall sounded like music to Alex's ears.

"Cool," he said in amazement. "Rich people even make something nice out of taking a dump."

Lessons

After lunch they walked slowly back to the beach and lay bloated in the sand. "How did you get to know her, anyway?" Alex asked.

"I told you already," said Robson. "At the beach."

"But how?"

"Just, you know. I asked her for money. So then she bought me a roll. She asked me all kinds of things too. Where I came from and stuff. After that she waved every time she was at the beach and saw me. Sometimes I'd go sit with her."

Alex kept silent. He hoped he would meet a lady like that on the beach too.

"She wants to adopt me," said Robson. "But there are still some things she has to fix up first."

"Mm-hmm," said Alex skeptically. "So are you going?"

"Of course I am. What would you do, man? A house. Food three times a day. A bed with sheets on it. Clean clothes. School. And …" He paused. "And a toilet with a supersonic flush."

Alex said nothing. "Then you'll be stuck with that kid," he blurted out.

"She's all right. Just like her mother. It's just because she doesn't know you," Robson said defensively.

"Then you'll have to be home on time," Alex started in again.

"Sure, because I have to get up at six-thirty in the morning to go to school. I bet I'll take the bus," said Robson. It sounded as if this appealed to him. "Guess what, she has a car too."

"And you thought the street was so fine. Come and go where you please," Alex taunted.

Robson looked at him. "You're jealous, man."

"Am not." Alex flopped over onto his other side.

Robson dreamed on. "If I were rich, I'd marry her."

"Who?"

"The girl—who else. Her mother?"

Alex opened his eyes wide and looked at the blue sky. Robson was wrong, he decided. He wasn't jealous. He wanted his mother back; yes, that was what he wanted.

They sat on the beach all afternoon.

At seven o'clock it grew dark and the floodlights switched on. They looked at the volleyball players setting up their nets. The beach looked like a sports field. On the path families strolled back and forth arm in arm. Among them zigzagged cyclists and joggers.

"Robson, what are those guys doing?" Alex pointed at the benches under the trees. It was dark there, but by the light of the moon you could see a boy sitting on every bench. Sometimes they got up, walked a few feet, then sat down again. There were also boys lying on the benches. "Do they sleep in the park too?"

Robson had to laugh. "No, they drop their pants and then they get money. Haven't you ever done that?"

"No," said Alex. He felt stupid.

"I have," said Robson.

"But who pays for that?"

"Men."

"Men?"

"Yeah, dirty old men with those bbbbrrrrr tongues." Robson stuck his tongue way out and let it flubber.

He was exaggerating, thought Alex.

Robson slapped him on the shoulder. "But you don't have to worry. Beanpoles like you have to pay."

Close to midnight they went to the brightly lit concrete band shell in the middle of the park. Robson insisted on sleeping there.

"But with all that light everybody can see you lying there," Alex protested.

"So what, stupid? Sleeping in the dark like you did, now that's dangerous. The more light, the better. Then they don't dare to come. Everybody can see you from the road, but they can see them too."

"Who's them?" asked Alex. Robson was a veteran; that much was clear.

"People who steal, kill, people who want to mess you up or rape you."

"Mess you up how?"

Robson took a deep breath. "You got people who get a kick out of roasting you alive. When you're asleep, they sneak up on you. They throw gasoline all over your blanket and then put a match to it. That burns like hell, man. Sadists is what they are. I slept at the Central Station for a week. It happens a lot there. You never saw that, kids with burns on their legs?"

"Well, it's a good thing we don't have a blanket," said Alex.

"Doesn't make any difference. They do it with plastic bags too. Set them on fire and then the plastic starts to drip. They hold that over you. Man, that hurts, if that stuff gets on your skin."

Alex kept silent. He chewed on his fingernails. He knew that the street was dangerous. But setting people on fire? How many nights would he have to keep going like this? He thought of what his stepfather had said. If you live on the street by yourself you'll die. Robson and himself, that was almost the same as being alone.

Robson spread out the newspaper he had brought along and sat down on it. "I got a surprise," he said.

Alex didn't react. He sat motionless on the steps with his plastic bag in his lap.

"Look." Robson pulled three marbles out of his pocket, one big one and two small ones. He wiped them clean on his T-shirt and gave two of them to Alex. "Here, you go first."

They played marbles until it got boring. Then they stretched out to sleep. Alex lay on his side and looked at the lights of the apartments of the *Flamengo* district. The road was nearby. Now and then he would see the lights of a passing car. Buzzing mosquitoes danced in front of the dome lights.

Robson coughed and rolled over.

"You asleep already?" Alex attempted carefully.

"Yeahhhh …" came from the other side.

"You're all right."

"As long as you don't start kissing me," grumbled Robson.

Alex snickered. "But I just have a thing for you."

"Gettawaaayyy," cried Robson. And they both laughed really hard.

Alex looked at the cloudless sky. He almost knew for sure—his mother had arranged Robson for him. "Thank you," he said softly to the sky.

It was a day later and Alex was sleeping next to Robson at the front of the park. That kid Robson knew everything and everybody in the park, he decided. Everybody said hello.

"Hey there, Robson, how you doing?"

"Fine, man."

Robson told Alex each time who the person he had talked to was. He knew the fishermen who had built their hut among the big rocks near the water. He knew exactly which park guards were cool and which ones liked to pull out their billy clubs. Those he called goons.

He also took Alex to meet Luís, the guard at the utility shed in the park. And of course he brought his new friend to see Dona Lica.

Dona Lica studied him from head to foot. "Weren't you sitting on that wall yesterday?" she asked.

Alex nodded and looked down at the ground.

"If there's any lifting to do, you can ask Alex too," Robson suggested.

Alex looked at him. Robson sure was generous. Sharing his job just like that.

Dona Lica was nice too, he decided. She let him give her his plastic bag with clothes. She would hang on to it.

"But I don't want any kind of trouble," she warned. "Stolen goods, drugs, or whatever. You keep them somewhere else."

Alex nodded.

Every day he and Robson hung around together. Alex was

surprised at how quickly he was becoming accustomed to life in the park. Only a couple of nights had passed and it felt like years. He and Robson were like two fingers on one hand. Dona Lica was already making jokes about it.

They spent hours on the pier that had been built on the beach out of huge blocks of stone. It extended forty yards out into the bay. There they sat with their feet in the water. Whenever a boat came by, they had to climb up quickly so as not to get soaked by the wake.

They played games, like who'd be the first to see a fish jump. Sometimes the fish leapt up six or seven feet. Robson said that was because the bay was polluted and they didn't get enough oxygen. Between the rocks there were crabs and mussels. These they cooked in an old tin can over a little fire. Sometimes they fished with a little string tied around an empty soft drink can and with scraps of food they found in the trash for bait.

Alex was happy that Robson didn't huff glue. He was scared of glue sniffers. He had made up his mind never to do that, no matter what happened. Maybe Robson had done it and quit. In any case, he never said anything about it. Alex didn't ask.

After the third time he ate at Vera's, Alex decided he wouldn't go to the apartment anymore. He felt ugly and dirty when he was there and the girl watched him eat every bite. He had the feeling that he was doing everything wrong.

Robson didn't understand. "Not go to Vera's anymore? It's good food, isn't it?"

"I don't want to mess up your chances," said Alex.

"You're not messing up my chances! Vera likes everybody."

"I'm still not going." Alex was determined. When he got something into his head, he was as stubborn as a mule.

"And how're you going to get food?" asked Robson.

"I'll figure out something," Alex said, sounding tough.

"Oh, come on, don't give me that! What am I supposed to say if they ask me where you are?" Robson insisted.

Alex grabbed him. "I feel ashamed, Robson. You got to understand that. They stare at me all the time. Because I don't eat like you. I got dirty clothes. I don't want to go."

Robson shrugged. "OK. Suit yourself."

That afternoon he came back with a plastic bag of food. "From Vera," he said.

Alex ate everything, down to the last grains of rice in the corner of the bag.

After that, Robson came back every day with food.

It was from Robson that Alex learned to panhandle. "Panhandling is normal," said Robson. "You're hungry and they got the money. It isn't your fault you don't have a home. So they have to help you."

Alex nodded. The way Robson explained it, panhandling actually seemed like work. The work street kids do. Still, he hoped he wouldn't run into anybody from Japeri. He'd die if they saw him holding out his hand.

One morning they went to a cantina, one of dozens on the street. You just walk in. They don't have any windows or doors, just roll-down metal shutters that go down to the ground and make a lot of noise when they're rolled up in the morning and dropped down at night. Most people stand at the counter and toss down a beer or a roll.

"Women are the best," Robson had said beforehand. "They're a lot more sympathetic. You walk over to her. Not too fast, because then she'll think you want to steal from her. When you're standing next to her, you say, 'Please, ma'am, don't you have some change for me? I'm so hungry.' Don't forget the part about being hungry. And you have to look pitiful." Robson had leaned his head a little to the side.

"And then she'll do it?" Alex had asked. He had often seen children panhandling but never knew it was so simple.

"Yeah, sometimes. If she doesn't do it right away but you can tell she wants to, you say, 'Ma'am, buy me a roll.' Some people don't want to give money. They think you're going to buy glue."

"What about men, don't they give money?"

"They do, sometimes." Robson had gotten caught up in his role as instructor. "Then there's people that want to get rid of you quick. They got fancy clothes on and they're scared you'll get them dirty. They give you money not to be bothered."

Alex was impressed by Robson. No wonder he was getting adopted. He knew exactly how to act.

Alex, who was able to put on a wide-eyed, innocent expression, turned out to be a good student. In half an hour he had picked up two *real*, enough for two Cokes and two rolls. Robson, who had been waiting farther down, must have slapped him on the back at least twenty times. "Damn! That's scoring, man."

When they got back that afternoon the wind started blowing. The fronds of the coconut palms rattled. The wind swept fallen leaves over the grass. Heavy clouds scudded over the bay and it grew dark.

"If you ask me, it's going to rain," said Alex.

Five minutes later the first fat drops began to come down. From the band shell the two boys watched drenched sunbathers scurry home through the park.

Alex drew boxes on the cement floor of the band shell with a stick. "You know," he said to Robson, continuing to draw. He waited for a moment. Would Robson be listening?

Robson was standing up, his mind somewhere else. "See that ship over there? Maybe it'll sink. You say something?" He turned around.

Alex took a deep breath. "You know, Robson—she wasn't my mother. She was my foster mother. She was white. But to me she's my mother. Because my real mother dumped me. I don't even know where she is."

Robson had sat down. "What the hell are you talking about, bitch?"

Alex took another breath. "About what I told you the first day. About my mother and the hospital. She's really my foster mother."

Robson looked at him searchingly. "Foster mother, sick mother, real mother—whoever takes care of you is your mother."

Alex stopped drawing. "Is that true?"

"Sure," said Robson. He slapped him on the back. "Let's go play marbles."

Alone Again

When Robson went to Vera's apartment, Alex usually stayed on the beach. Sometimes he helped Dona Lica. One day Robson came back all excited.

"I can go live with her."

Alex was shocked. Suddenly he felt the wet towel again that made his heart heavy.

"I get to have my own room, man. And she already talked to the head of the school. Maybe I'll even be starting next week. That's fly, don't you think?" Robson was hopping from one foot to the other. He rattled on and on. Alex had never seen him so happy.

"You lucked out," said Alex, but it sounded flat.

Robson looked at him. "Hey, man, don't feel bad. I'm sure you'll run into somebody that wants to adopt you, too."

"If I'm still alive." Alex's voice hitched in his throat. But he meant it.

That afternoon Robson left for the bed with the sheets on it. They shook hands. They had never done that. It was done solemnly, the way men take leave of one another.

Alex hadn't cried. He never cried, but he felt lonely afterward. Even more than he had the first night in the park. He hung around until midnight watching people play soccer and then slowly walked down the asphalt bike path through the park to the brightly lit band shell.

There were plastic cups lying around and a half-eaten hamburger in a paper bag. He sat down on the steps and reflected. There was the sound of voices in the distance. Somebody laughed. It was the late-night volleyball players going home. The sound slowly faded away. What remained was the buzzing of insects in the lights, and now and then the pattering of a twig falling or the dull roar of a passing car. He lay down on the bare concrete. His plastic bag was at Dona Lica's and he had forgotten to find a newspaper. Dust tickled his throat and a piece of grit pricked his cheek. Alex wanted to go to sleep, but his thoughts flew through his mind like a whirlwind. There was one that kept coming back: out of here. He had to get out of here quickly. He had to find somebody, just as Robson had, to adopt him.

A twig fell. And another. No, that couldn't be twigs. Somebody was walking around. He lifted himself up and looked at the bushes. Had he seen something move? He had the feeling that somebody was spying on him. What was that? Yes, now he was certain. Rustling and panting. What should he do? His heart was pounding in his throat. He wanted to run away. But where to? Where was he safe? Something Robson had said flashed through his mind. The more light, the better. He took a deep breath and shouted at the bushes, "Beat it. I know you're—

you're … there." It didn't come out exactly the way he wanted it to, but he was satisfied anyway. It gave him a sense of relief.

But when he lay down again, his doubts returned. Who was going to listen to a thirteen-year-old boy wearing torn shorts and a dirty T-shirt?

If only he had four walls around him. Then he'd rest easy. Not even a house. Just four walls. Alex thought of the wall in his bedroom in Japeri. The red bricks, called breeze blocks because they had more air in them than clay, and the window where he'd hung a piece of carpeting so the rain wouldn't get in. Would Bruno have the bed to himself now?

He shifted around. His legs were white from the concrete. He slowly drifted off.

A night has a thousand hours when you live on the street. Especially when you're all alone. After Robson left, Alex slept badly. Every morning at six o'clock when the sun came up his heart leapt; the night was over. During the day he caught up on his sleep. Beneath the palm trees near the bike path or on the beach beside Dona Lica's shed. But usually the day flew by and then it was night again.

He didn't see Robson anymore. Maybe he was going to school now. Since Vera's food parcels had stopped coming, getting enough to eat had become more complicated. When he wasn't sleeping, he was busy doing that. In the morning he sometimes went to the cantina across the street from the park to ask for food. But he still didn't have Robson's nerve. He was ashamed to ask. Many times he would be standing there and at the last minute he would ask for water. Everybody gave you water. That wasn't begging.

He hauled boxes of cans and heavy sacks of coconuts for Dona Lica. She sometimes gave him one or two *real*. For two *real*, a lady who sat by the footpath sold hot food in plastic containers. If there wasn't anything else, he went to the pier to look for mussels.

He often sat on the rocks. He liked that spot. Nobody else scrambled all the way to the end. Nobody on the beach could see you anymore. Sometimes he'd wash his shorts and T-shirt in the water so that they could dry out on the stones. The point was his uninhabited island. He pretended the bay was the ocean. He was waiting for a ship that would pick him up. What was that man's name again—Robinson Crusoe or Cruzo?

He decided it was Crusoe. If anybody asked him what his name was, he would say Crusoe. That was how he felt: on an island, all alone.

He spent hours on the pier. He talked to the fish and the waves. The stray cats were tigers. Behind the trees he saw monkeys running around. Whenever a boat passed, he would wave. Then they could come rescue him. But they never saw him, a little speck among the blocks of stone.

When it started to get dark he would climb up and go to the band shell. To that other island. The island of light in the dark park.

"Hey, aren't you Robson's friend?"

Alex was lying in the sand, asleep, when he heard a voice from far away. Then he felt a hand on his back. He jumped. They were coming to get him.

"Aren't you Robson's friend?" he heard.

Blinking in the light, he looked up. First he saw hairy brown legs, then striped swimming trunks with a small roll of bills at the height of the hip bone, and after that a face that looked familiar. It was a man Robson knew who had once bought soda and chips for them.

"Well, well. Back in the land of the living?"

Alex smiled back shyly.

"Where's your friend?"

"Robson's living in an apartment," Alex replied. "He was adopted and he's going to school."

"Well, nooww," said the man. He drew out the *ow* and meanwhile studied Alex from head to toe. "So now you're all alone?"

"Mm-hmm," said Alex. And he thought: If this guy keeps it up, I'm out of here. He looked at Dona Lica, but she was waving her arms around, talking with two ladies taking a walk, and she hadn't noticed anything.

The man placed his sandals side by side on the sand and sat down on them, next to Alex. "So, you live on the street?"

What did he mean, so? thought Alex. What did he know about it? But Alex said, "Yeah, something like that." He made up his mind not to provide any more answers. This guy was like a cop, just about.

"That can't be easy," the man continued. "Did your stepfather kick you out of the house?"

Alex was surprised. How could he know that? "Yeah, more or less," he replied. "My mother died. But I was only half living at home really. After she went into the hospital I spent a lot of time with friends." That last part was a lie, because although he had slept at friends' houses, during the day he had wandered the streets. What did the man know.

"Losing your mother is the worst thing that can happen to you. That's when you're really alone. The love and support she gives you can't compare with anything else," the man said.

Alex's jaw dropped. This man was saying it exactly the way he himself felt. He was all right, Alex decided.

The man checked his watch. "I'm not your mother, but non-mothers can sometimes cook pretty nice, too. I'm going home to eat. I'm sure you're hungry. If you want to come along, it's no problem."

In surprise, Alex looked up. Of course he wanted to go, but was he really to be trusted? He thought of Robson's scary old men. "Do you live by yourself?"

The man shook his head. "No, I live with my nephew. You don't have to be afraid."

They went by cab, the man in his swimming trunks and Alex with his plastic bag. Because he could take a shower there, too, the man had said.

"My name's Vasco," said the man. "And yours?"

"Crusoe," replied Alex and he quickly looked out the window again. He had never sat in a car before, but he wasn't really able to enjoy it. He felt uncomfortable with this almost naked man beside him.

They drove through streets of old houses with façades that looked like frosted cakes. There were lots of garages and antique stores and it was busy. The sidewalks were full of stands and pedestrians.

"Look, Crusoe, the samba stadium." The man gave him a nudge.

Alex looked and saw high concrete bleachers and a street in between. They drove right through the middle.

Vasco lived close to the samba stadium. The doorman wasn't sitting behind glass but outside on a chair. Everything wasn't as fancy as at Vera's, but it was still much nicer looking than Japeri.

"There's the shower," Vasco said, pointing, when they were upstairs in the apartment. "Black beans—you like them, I hope?"

Alex had to laugh. Anybody who didn't like black beans didn't like eating.

When he came out of the shower, there were steaming dishes on the table. "Dig in, I'm sure you're hungry," said Vasco. "I'm going to jump into the shower."

Alex had almost finished his plate when Vasco returned, wearing a white bathrobe.

"Was it all right?"

Alex nodded.

"If you want, Crusoe, you can always eat here," said Vasco. He served Alex another helping.

Alex nodded enthusiastically because speaking was impossible. His mouth was full.

"You can live here if you want. There's enough room."

This time the spoon remained suspended halfway to Alex's mouth. He gasped for breath. "Do you mean that?"

"Yes, otherwise I wouldn't say it. It's ridiculous, really—you on the street when I've got extra rooms here."

Alex actually thought so too. "But what about your nephew?"

Vasco was briefly disconcerted. "He'll think it's a good idea too," he said finally. "A fine boy like you. Who could have any objection to that?" He got up and approached Alex. "I know for sure, Crusoe, that we'll get along just fine." He laid both hands on Alex's shoulders and squeezed.

Alex choked. He started to cough like crazy. The beans shot up into his nose.

"Easy, boy. Easy," said Vasco. He patted him on the back. But Alex kept coughing and gasping for breath.

Vasco ran to the kitchen and returned with some water. Alex was out of breath. His head was hot. How was he going to get out of here?

"Drink some of this," said Vasco, pointing at the glass in front of him. Alex drank and looked at the door out of the corner of his eye. The key was in it. Vasco hadn't locked him in.

"Thank you very much," he said after he had emptied the glass. The half-finished plate he pushed away.

"Come on, stand up," said Vasco.

Alex didn't dare refuse. He pushed his chair back and was about to stand up. But then he saw Vasco. He had let his bathrobe slip off and was standing there stark naked on a cloud of white terry cloth.

Alex grabbed hold of the table. "Uh, I need to be going," he mumbled. "And uh … thank you very much for the hospitality." He looked at the door again. How many steps would it take for him to be outside?

"What's all this about?" said Vasco. "Won't you stay and listen to some music? I thought we were friends." He bent down for his robe.

Alex noticed out of the corner of his eye that Vasco had hair on his butt. "I got to meet somebody," Alex fabricated. He braced himself. If this guy kept on whining, he'd have to kick him.

"Weeelll," said Vasco. He had thrown his bathrobe on again and was staring at him intently. "This can all be yours, Alex. If you come live here, you can go to school and there's always food to eat."

"I got to meet somebody," Alex repeated. His head was so hot that he couldn't think up anything else. He took a step toward the door.

"All right," Vasco continued. He suddenly sounded a lot more stern. "But remember one thing, boy. Anybody who lives on the street by himself is condemned to death."

"I got to meet somebody," said Alex, very loudly this time. He took another step.

"All right, all right." Vasco walked in front of him quickly. As Alex walked out the door, he took hold of his arm for an instant. "Here, boy. This is for you."

He tucked a rolled-up banknote into Alex's hand.

Bad Dream

Whether he was running in the right direction Alex didn't know anymore. He ran as fast as he could. He had slipped the banknote into his pocket. Later he would check to see how much it was. First he had to get away from that creepy guy.

"Hey, you little punk, watch where you're going," cried an old man he had almost knocked down.

But Alex heard nothing. He ran this way and that among the people on the crowded sidewalk. He didn't notice that every-body was staring at him. Some of the pedestrians flattened themselves against the building fronts as if they were afraid he was going to touch them.

Suddenly he felt a hand on his upper arm. He tugged and tugged. But his arm was held in a vise grip. "Let me go!" At the same time he heard the screeching of brakes. Suddenly people were crowding around him. He didn't have a clue about what was going on. Had there been an accident?

An officer with his pistol drawn pushed people to the side. "Stand aside. We'll take care of this." A second officer swung the door of the patrol car shut. "Thank you," said the first officer to the passerby who was gripping Alex's arm. He let him go.

But immediately he felt a new, cold hand in his neck.

"Walk, pal." The next instant he was smacked up against a wall. A knee was shoved into his behind. His cheek scraped on the stones.

"Hands up. C'mon, against the wall."

Like a sleepwalker, Alex did as he was told. He felt hands pass along his crotch and underneath his T-shirt. He tried to look sideways, but a hand immediately pressed his forehead flat against the wall. What were people saying? Was he hearing right?

"Street kid? Street thief, you mean."

"As young as they are, they're already walking around armed."

"If you don't watch out, wham, you've got a knife in your gut."

One of the officers grabbed him under his armpit and turned him around. "Papers?"

"Don't have any, sir." Alex felt his body burn. This was really bad.

"Why did you take off? Are you training for the Olympics?"

"I, uh … he wanted to …" Alex thought feverishly. What was he supposed to say? They wouldn't believe it. Or worse, they'd cry "Queer!" and beat him up and rape him.

"Who is 'he'?" asked the officer impatiently and squeezed his armpit even tighter.

"That man on the beach. Va … Vasco," stammered Alex.

The officer turned to his partner, who had stood there listening. "Take him in," the partner said.

The officer standing next to Alex took the handcuffs hanging on his belt and clicked them around Alex's wrists. "We're going to have to have a little talk, pal." He shoved him into the patrol car that was parked halfway on the sidewalk.

Alex caught a glimpse of the cherries on top, still flashing. He was shaking all over. He had been walking around on the planet long enough to know that this "little talk" from the mouth of a police officer didn't mean anything good. A policeman is a thug in a uniform, they said in Japeri.

On the back seat, separated from the front seat by a metal grille, he asked God, and, just to make sure, his mother as well, if he could please be allowed to live. And preferably not get beaten up either.

They brought him to an empty lot close to the samba stadium. He had to get out of the car and stand up against a wall. One of the officers gave him a slap in the face with the flat of his hand, so hard he almost fell over. The other one kicked him in the crotch.

"Cut it out! I didn't do anything," Alex screamed. He felt the pain shoot through his groin.

"And giving orders too," said the first officer. "Watch your mouth, punk. Turn around and put your hands on your head."

Alex did so. Then he felt hands in his pockets.

"Here, ten *real*," he heard one of them say.

Jesus, he thought. Vasco had given him a whole ten *real* and those bastards were taking it away from him.

"Nothing else?" the other one asked.

"No, what should we do? What time is it?"

Alex heard the officers talking. He didn't dare turn around. As long as they didn't take him with them.

The first officer stepped over to him and turned him around. He had drawn his pistol. The barrel was aimed at Alex. "You see this, freeloader? Liar that you are. Next time, you're dead."

He turned around and the next minute the car jounced back onto the pavement and disappeared around a corner. Alex watched. He hated them.

He walked back to the park, but his legs were heavy and his head was pounding.

That night he had a dream. Officers with clubs were standing around him. One of them stepped forward and pulled out his pistol. The black barrel was like a hollow eye three feet away from him. There were lots of people jeering, "Street kid, street thief, street kid, street thief." Then it was quiet for a second. He heard a voice. It was his stepfather's voice, but he couldn't see him. "You're a thief. You, nothing but lies. You're condemned to death, Alex dos Santos." The voice laughed. A gurgling, wheezy laugh. The officer with the pistol cocked the trigger.

"No! I'm not who you think I am," Alex screamed. Then he bolted awake.

"Ghuu, ghuuu." On the steps of the band shell sat the bum from the first night. He was laughing, but it seemed more like coughing. "Ghuuu, ghuuueh, friend. Easy. I only asked you if you had a swig of something to drink."

"Didn't you notice anything last night, then?" asked Dona Lica when he walked up the beach the following morning. "A boy got shot and killed. A bullet through his head. Luís called the police right away. But the body's still lying there, since last night. If it's a fancy street or if there's a hotel nearby then they'll pick it up in half an hour. But somewhere else it can just lie there for half a day and rot in the sun. You know Luís, don't you? The utility shed guard?"

Alex nodded. Luís was one of Robson's friends.

"Well, he was on duty last night. He looked over the top of the fence when he heard the shots. He said he saw two of them. If you ask me, it was to get even."

Alex was only half listening. His thoughts were flitting around. A boy shot dead. In the park. So something like that was possible. Nobody had prevented it. Maybe he would be next. There were killers wandering the park. Killers.

Dona Lica had said something about that. "To get even, Dona Lica? But who?" asked Alex.

"Don't ask me." Dona Lica threw up her hands. "My God, nowadays you get shot just for looking a little too long at somebody else's wife." She leaned forward. "I didn't say anything about Luís. You don't know anything. Later on they'll be picking Luís up, poor guy. Ai-ai, what a world we live in."

Dona Lica was scared. That's why she didn't want to say more. Alex was sure of it. "Oh, come on, Dona Lica," he insisted. "What do you mean, get even?"

Dona Lica looked around quickly. "Come here," she said and she pulled Alex closer. "He was an *aviao*. You know what that is, don't you?"

Alex nodded. An *aviao* was a runner, a guy who carried packets of drugs for dealers in the city. Sometimes to clients. Sometimes from one selling spot to another. Mostly that went on in the ghetto.

"They say he snitched about something. The police had followed him. They gave him a hard time and then he dropped a name. They say. Those drug dealers are no sweethearts. Friends that talk a little too much, a runner that knows too much—it all ends up thisaway." Dona Lica drew her index finger quickly across her throat.

Alex heaved a sigh.

"C'mon, boy." Dona Lica threw her arms around him. "I know you're a good boy. But, for God's sake, watch out. Don't get in with that kind. You know what I mean, right? There's a man who walks around here in the park every day asking boys like you to pick up a package. Once you're in, boy … it's playing with fire. But, hey, give me a hand now with the beer."

Later, when Alex was walking through the park, he passed the spot where the murder had taken place. There were a few park guards and some sunbathers standing around. The boy lay on the ground. Somebody had spread a newspaper out over him, but his legs were half sticking out. They were black legs covered with the scars of burns. He started. The boy was wearing the same plastic flip-flops he was.

Duda

After the shooting, Alex didn't dare sleep in the park. He went back to the spot he knew best: the Central Station. After all, he used to come here every day when he was still selling cookies on the train. Now, when the trains stopped running at midnight, he would climb over the shunting yard fence, push open a train car door, and find himself a wooden seat. In the morning, as it was beginning to get light, he would slip away. By about six the railroad cops would come and beat everybody.

At night he wasn't the only one on the train. The fourth night he woke up because there was somebody hanging over him. He felt a hand in his pockets. Through the slits of his eyes Alex saw a black man with a knife in his left hand. The blade glinted in the moonlight. Alex pretended to be asleep. He knew he would lose. The hands found the five-*real* note he had on him. Through his eyelashes he saw the man leave. He wanted to cry, but he had no tears. Only toward morning did he fall asleep.

That day he met Duda. He had picked up his plastic bag at Dona Lica's and was washing his T-shirt and shorts in a fountain right by the movie theaters. She had a pile of dirty clothes.

"You live on the street too?" she asked while they were sitting on the stone rim of the fountain and the clothes were hanging out to dry on the fence.

"I sleep on the trains," said Alex.

Duda looked at him questioningly. "You down with the Platform Panthers?"

"The what?"

"The Platform Panthers," she repeated. "The Central Station gang."

"Nooo," said Alex. That was the truth. He didn't know anything about any gang.

"Oh, then it's OK. They're our enemies. We're the Asphalt Angels."

Alex only half understood, but he clicked his tongue to indicate something like "I see."

When she asked him what his name was, he said, "Crusoe."

"Cruzo?" Duda was looking at him searchingly, as if she thought it was a funny name. "Cruzo," she repeated slowly. As if she wanted to taste the name on her tongue.

"Crusoe," Alex corrected her.

She ignored that. "I'm Eduarda. But they call me Duda."

Alex looked at her out of the corner of his eye. Duda didn't look at all like someone who lived on the street. She was light brown and had sleek, short black hair. She was wearing earrings and sneakers instead of flip-flops. Her clothes were new. He thought she was really kind of pretty. She was big, too.

"How old are you?" he asked her.

"You don't ask a lady that." Duda laughed and walked over to the fence to check the laundry.

"Do you wear men's clothes?"

"Lord, so many questions. No, they're my husband's."

Ow, thought Alex, if she was married, she had to be old. Maybe she was eighteen already.

It was as if she had read his thoughts. "I've been married since I was twelve."

Alex's jaw dropped. He had made it with a girl for the first time when he was eleven. But married at twelve? "Since you were twelve?" he asked.

"Sure, why not? If you die quick, you got to marry quick, too."

Pffft, thought Alex. She was acting like he was a baby and she was a woman of the world. But he still thought she was nice.

It was a day later when he saw Duda again. "Cruzo, Cruzo!" she shouted. Alex was sitting on a bench in the square across from the fountain. He had slept there the previous night. After being robbed he didn't want to go back to the trains. The square with the movie theaters and restaurants was busy, lit up and noisy until far into the night. That spelled safety. Robson had been right. Alex saw that more clearly every day. Wasn't for nothing that other people slept in the square too.

"Listen, Cruzo," said Duda when she was standing beside the stone bench, "this is Roy, my husband." She pointed at the guy she was with, a tough-looking type who was white and wearing a T-shirt with elephants on it. There was a yellow Walkman dangling from his pants.

"My name's Crusoe, not Cruzo," Alex said firmly.

"OK, Crusoe. This is my husband."

"Listen, Crusoe," said the tough-looking type. "We need

some dough. We want to buy a can."

"A can?"

"Yeah, a can of glue, man. Five *real*, you got five *real*?"

Alex looked at the outstretched hand.

"Hey, man. Don't give me a hard time," said Roy. "Out here on the street everybody's everybody's friend. We help each other out. Bad off together is less bad off." He laughed loudly at his own joke. "Anybody not your friend is your enemy," he added. It sounded like a threat.

Alex felt around in his pocket. He had earned three *real* at Dona Lica's yesterday afternoon. One he had spent on a sandwich last night. These two he had saved for breakfast. He was always hungriest in the morning. "So how am I supposed to eat?" he sputtered.

"I'll pay you back tomorrow," Roy reassured him.

It was a lie, Alex thought. He would never get the money back. Once given, gone forever. Reluctantly he handed over his two *real*.

"Only two *real*?" Roy said as he took the bills.

"What's your problem? Do I look like a millionaire?" Alex responded with irritation.

This evidently made an impression, because Roy said nothing. He turned away.

"Ciao," said Duda and she waved enthusiastically. It made Alex feel a little better.

When he returned from a round at the cantina, where he had panhandled enough for breakfast, he saw Duda and her friends right away. They were sitting on the grass by the fountain huffing glue. They were holding plastic bags or soda cans in their hands. It looked as if they were drinking, but Alex knew they were inhaling. He sat on a stone bench and hoped they hadn't seen him. If they got good and crazy from huffing, they could stab him to death or beat him up.

But on the grass they seemed to be having a good time. They lay against one another, rolled in the grass. Now and then they'd get up and dance around.

On the street, kids sleep in groups. That's safer. While one is asleep, another can stand guard. Duda and Roy's group numbered six. They slept in a covered arcade along the sidewalk in Santa Luzia Street, right near the square. They pooped in a little plot of greenery nearby and they showered at night in the fountain on the square. Since he had given money, Alex was now almost part of the group.

"You want to eat?" Duda asked the next day.

Her friends were sitting on the grass near the fountain with aluminum foil containers in their laps. Roy held up a drumstick glistening with grease. "Hey, how's my man?"

Alex was annoyed. "And yesterday you guys didn't have any money!"

"Roy was at it early," Duda said proudly. "Twenty *real* and it isn't even noon yet." She gave Alex a drumstick from her container.

"How'd he do that?" asked Alex.

"Jacked two bags. One from an old lady on the corner over there by the consulate, and one from a man who was waiting for the bus."

"The guy was so scared, he gave me his bag before I could say anything," Roy added.

"What do you expect? Have you ever looked at yourself before noon?" said one of the eaters, grinning. "Man, that dracula-head even scares me."

"With the rest we can huff." A kid with light cat's eyes shoved Roy. "Hey, boss, how about some huffy-huff?"

"If you go get it, Huff," said Roy. "I got the day off now." He worked down a last bite of rice and threw the empty container over his shoulder into the bushes. Then he motioned to a kid— the youngest, as far as Alex could tell—with bleached hair.

"Hey, Scissors, go buy me a bottle of Coke. And I want the change back." Roy waved a banknote.

"But I haven't finished eating," the kid protested. He gave Roy an imploring look.

His neighbor took advantage of his moment of inattention and snatched the aluminum container out of his lap, then ran across the square.

"Son of a bitch! Bastard! Wimp!" The boy who had been addressed as Scissors exploded into profanities. Then he threw himself with clenched fists on Roy and started pounding him. "It's your fault, pukeface!" Passersby looked in astonishment at the two bodies rolling in the grass.

"Pukeface, who's the pukeface here?" Roy twisted Scissors' right arm behind his back, spit in his face, and let him go.

Scissors took his defeat without batting an eye, wiped his cheek with his left shoulder, and looked across the square. The thief was sitting on a cement bench eating. When he saw Scissors, he waved cheerfully.

Scissors exploded again. "I'll kill him, that bastard!" And he ran across the street right in front of the honking cars.

Alex turned to Roy. He was the oldest. Would he interfere? But Roy had shifted his attention to Duda. She was lying down with her head in his lap. He ran his hands through her hair and kissed her now and then. They seemed to have forgotten the rest of the world.

What strange friendships these kids have, thought Alex. They'll bash each other's heads in over a plate of food.

Asphalt Angels

On the street, hardly anybody goes by their real name. In Duda's group there was Bocão, whose real name was Alberto. He was the one who had snatched Scissors' food. Bocão, or Big Mouth, was fourteen and just as black as Alex. Every Friday night Big Mouth disappeared. He would go to raves in the ghettos where they played loud rap music.

Big Mouth had two hobbies: rap and picking up girls. Every Saturday morning he would come back with juicy stories. "All those whores want a rapper," said Big Mouth. "We got more experience." Experience in what he didn't say.

Alex had seen from his clothes that Big Mouth was a rapper. He wore baggy shorts and a baseball cap and he had flashy white sneakers. He washed them every day.

Big Mouth had a mother and two younger brothers. Who his

father was he didn't know. He had gone to school for three years and then quit. Go sell pens, his mother had said. Because at home they were poor. The only thing they had was an old fridge held shut with a piece of string. It was always empty.

Big Mouth sold stuff downtown. He had to catch two buses to get home. When he didn't have much money, he slept on the street. After he discovered rap music, he stayed away on the weekends too. One day he didn't go back at all. "Why should I?" he said when he was telling Alex his story. "There's nothing there anyway."

Carlos' nickname was Chincheiro, Huff. No other name would have suited him better. Huff thought all day about huffing. He sniffed glue and snorted cocaine. "You die anyhow. At least this way you're having a good time while it lasts," he said.

Huff was sixteen and light brown, with light-colored eyes. He walked with a bit of a stoop. He didn't know who his father was, and his mother was always off somewhere. He hated her. "She killed my littlest sister," he told Alex one day. The baby had been found smothered in a cloth in the courtyard.

Huff lived with his older sister at his grandma's. But she couldn't handle him. He skipped school and stole. One day the gas bottle disappeared from the kitchen, which put an end to cooking. Grandma had cried and Huff had promised to do better. One day Huff borrowed the neighbor boy's bike and returned the following day without it. He said it had been stolen, but nobody believed his story.

That same evening three boys showed up at the door. They were armed. Everybody in the neighborhood knew that they worked for the local dealer. Because he had a lot of guns, the dealer was the boss in the neighborhood. He decided who could build a house, who was on the neighborhood committee, who got into the neighborhood and who didn't. Even the police were scared of him. If there were any disputes among the neighbors, he decided who was right. Anybody who got in his way he shot dead.

The dealer decided Huff needed a lesson. "You don't steal from your own people. Stealing you do outside the 'hood. I don't want any trouble or cops here," he had said. He gave Huff a choice: a bullet through both hands, or disappear. If he ever set foot in the neighborhood again, he would be shot and killed. Huff left.

The little kid was Tesourinho, Scissors. Nobody knew what his real name was. He was called Scissors because he was knock-kneed. Scissors was ten. But you gave him eight at the most because he was small and skinny. He wore old T-shirts that came down to below his knees like dresses. Alex had a soft spot for Scissors. He reminded him of Bruno.

Scissors sniffed glue, was as agile as an acrobat, and loved cartoons. Sometimes he would sit for hours on the sidewalk, like a little human heap among the many hurrying legs, in front of the display window of an electronics store where televisions were turned on. He often didn't even notice people running into him. Sucking on his thumb, he was in another world, that of *The Lion King. The Lion King* was his favorite animated film. Scissors had asked Duda to bleach his nappy hair because then he would look more like a lion. When he was cheerful, Scissors would run around the street, his arms mowing through the air and his head stretched forward. "Grrrrrrrrrrrr, the lion's out, the lion's out!" he would yell. He had no idea that people followed him with their eyes and shook their heads.

Scissors had lived on the street all his life, first in Copacabana with his mother and three brothers and sisters. His father had run off, and his mother hadn't had the money to pay rent. Because there were lots of tourists in Copacabana and people with money, they had gone there on the bus. His mother had built a hut out of cardboard on the sidewalk, and as soon as little Scissors was able to walk she sent him out panhandling at the stoplights. Scissors liked the street. The people, the noise, and the light. He was always ready for anything. That was also how he had started sniffing glue. When his mother found out, she hit him. "Boy, you're ruined. You'll go to the devil." That evening, when they were all sleeping, Scissors took to his heels. He was seven then.

Because he was the youngest in the group, Scissors was often sent out to steal. "They won't arrest you," said Roy.

Then there was Pera, Pear, whose real name was José. He was thirteen like Alex and black. At first Alex thought Pear was a girl. Pear walked like a girl, talked like a girl, and looked like a girl. He didn't wear long baggy shorts but, like a girl, tight short shorts. And Pear would cut the sleeves off all his T-shirts so that they looked a little like a girl's tank tops. His toenails he painted red.

José had been "Pear" from his first day with the group. Because on the street, women were called pears. Pear had been thrown out of his house because he talked funny. "You act normal or you get the hell out," his father had said. So Pear had left.

Pear let himself be grabbed behind cars by men. Sometimes they would take him along to the park. For that he got money. Pear was friendly with a waiter who worked in a restaurant on the square. He would let Pear into the kitchen through the back door when there weren't many customers. In the employees' bathroom he would have to suck the guy's dick. After that he would get a plate of food.

Everybody made jokes about Pear. "Hey, fag. Look at them big tits." And: "How about a round for everybody?" But Pear could count on Duda's help. "Bunch of punks," Duda would say, looking scornful. Then the teasing would stop at once.

Nobody wanted to be on Duda's wrong side. Anybody who did got Roy on their case. Because Roy was there, Duda could sleep among the boys.

There weren't a lot of girls on the street. The few who wandered around always hung together. Alex could see the sense in that. Boys couldn't keep their hands to themselves. Duda didn't have to worry about that, since Roy was jealous. "Keep your paws off my wife," he would shout if the others were leaning up against Duda too much for his liking. He made an exception only in Pear's case because the gang thought of Pear as a girl.

Duda played mother to them all. She was the one who settled arguments and took care of injuries. She would often visit with the mothers who lived with their children in the square.

Duda was sixteen and a half. She had run away from home because her father was always groping her, and her mother did nothing about it. The first months after she had run away she had slept on line 638. That's the bus that runs day and night. Most of the drivers said nothing when she ducked under the turnstile so as not to have to pay and sat through three or four runs. Sometimes she would sit in the back. You could lie down better on the back seat, but it was more dangerous. That's where the drunks, the street rappers, and the pickpockets sat, because they didn't go through the turnstile. During the day when she knew for sure that her father wasn't around, she would go home to get clean clothes, eat, and sometimes catch up on sleep. Just after her twelfth birthday she had had a boyfriend who lived on the street. She had stayed with him until he left her for someone else. That was what Alex had heard. Now she was with Roy.

They were always kissing, wherever and whenever. On the grass, on the beach, in between the cars, on benches in the square, and of course at night. Then Roy would dive under Duda's T-shirt. Duda would giggle and the others would turn away. They were at it again. If you looked over after a time, they would be so entangled that you couldn't tell anymore whose arm or leg was whose.

Duda admired Roy. She washed his clothes, cut his hair, popped his zits, and pulled ticks out of his hair. In short, she really was his wife.

Nobody knew much about Roy, maybe because he had been on the street the longest. And he never talked about the past and nobody asked him about it. Roy was the boss. He was what you would call a street father. He bought the food and he always knew how they could get glue or cocaine. He decided what the gang was going to do and gave the orders. The others accepted that.

Roy was nineteen and knew the ways of the world. He knew the hustlers at the Central Station, the guys you could sell stolen watches to. He knew which police officers you could trust and which ones you couldn't. He was friendly with "the people in the business," as drug dealers were referred to on the street.

What he did, exactly, Alex didn't know. But he had once seen that some high roller's son had come driving up in his dad's car. He had given Roy money because he didn't dare go into the ghetto with his flossy car to buy cocaine. Roy had then sent Huff off. How did that guy know, Alex had wondered, that Roy had contacts in the drug business?

Roy arranged to get glue through a panhandler or a carwasher. It had to be that way because only adults with an ID could buy glue. Roy had no papers, so he was out. A few of the carwashers or panhandlers would do the job for a commission.

Roy had also thought up the name of the crew. Asphalt Angels. The group had not gone along with it without some resistance.

"Angels?" Duda questioned. "But we're no angels."

"It's straight because it has something hard and something soft to it," Roy, who was quite taken with his idea, had replied.

"We sleep on stoops, not on asphalt," protested Scissors.

Huff had suggested Santa Luzia Rebels.

Pear, who usually kept quiet during discussions of this sort while squeezing pimples or cleaning under his nails, had also had a proposal: God Be With Us.

Huff needed little persuasion. "That's what the dope dealers of the Red Commando are called too." The Red Commando was a bunch of gangsters that dealt not only in drugs but also in weapons. They had a lot of power in the city.

"God, no. We can't have trouble," Duda said in alarm.

"Do you want God not to be with us?" asked Pear. Everybody nodded in agreement but didn't dare to say anything more.

It had remained Asphalt Angels. Roy was the boss after all.

On the Street

The wind was blowing. Old newspapers and scraps of paper danced across the bare pavement. An empty beer can rattled into the gutter. Alex stared at the water stains in the roof of the Santa Luzia Street arcade. Every night he slept with the Asphalt Angels. Like everybody else he kept his things in the dry manhole in the sidewalk. Nobody questioned him. Friends come and friends go.

"Think it's going to rain?" asked Huff. Huff was lying beside him. They were the only ones on the bed of cardboard who were awake. Big Mouth was lying stiffly against Pear. He had thrown his arm around Pear and was snoring loudly. Scissors was a bump under a gray rag. Because he was the littlest, he had the only blanket, one that Roy had snatched from a drunk bum. He had pulled it up over his head. On the other side lay Duda and Roy, intimately entwined as usual.

"I didn't see any clouds tonight," whispered Alex. He raised his head, but they were lying against the wall and from that part of the arcade you couldn't see the sky.

"What month is it?" Huff wanted to know.

Alex was shocked to discover that he didn't know either. It was winter when he left home. How many weeks had he been living on the street now? Was the rainy season over already? "I don't know," he said at last.

Alex was lying on the outside. Every night the boys spread out a couple of pieces of cardboard and the first one to lie down had the best spot. Which was to say the very best spot—in the middle—was for Scissors because he was the littlest. In the middle it was safe. Alex had been slow to move. If the cops came to chase them out, he'd be the one that got kicked. That was his lot as outfielder. Or if those sadists spilled their bottles of gasoline all over them, he'd be the first to be on fire. But whoever was lying on the outside was also the first one to be able to run away.

Alex mulled this over, since he couldn't fall asleep. In the distance he heard a car pull up. Then it was quiet again. The street looked a lot wider now that it was empty. The cantinas, the barbershop, and the travel agency in the gallery were all hidden behind metal shutters. The glass doors of the office building, open in the daytime, were dark mirrors.

Against one of the marble pillars of the arcade leaned a garbage bag that the doorman from one of the buildings had set down before catching the night bus home. Suddenly Alex saw a cockroach. It was as big as his little finger, and its red-brown armored back gleamed. It came out from under the garbage bag and ran across the black and white tiles of the stoop toward him. Alex wanted to cry out, but at the last minute his attacker veered away and disappeared down a crack between the tiles. Alex breathed a sigh of relief.

A man appeared around the corner. Alex opened his eyes wide. But no, they didn't have anything to worry about from guys of that kind. Judging from his uncertain gait, he was drunk. After a couple of steps he stood still. He reached his hand out toward the wall. When he had found it he unzipped his fly. Alex watched a little stream crinkle over the stoop.

Pear moved. He freed himself from Big Mouth's embrace and disappeared in the direction of the museum. On the side of the museum was some shrubbery, which they used as a bathroom at night. During the day, when there were more people out, they went between the cars parked in an alley.

From the direction of the square a squad car came driving up. It drove very slowly along the sidewalk, the headlights turned off. Alex saw the barrel of an automatic sticking out of the window. His heart stopped. This was it.

"Huff," he whispered. "Huff, wake up."

But Huff didn't respond. What was the best thing to do, Alex wondered—act like you're sleeping or shout for everybody to wake up and run away? He chose, more from cowardice than anything else, the first option and squeezed his eyes to slits. The car drove on by.

Alex heard the Central Station clock chime four o'clock. Shortly after that he fell asleep. The wind had died down.

At six o'clock, when the custodian of the bar turned on the hose, he finally woke up.

Every morning around six the Asphalt Angels left for the square. Usually they slept there in the grass near the fountain or on the stone benches. That was part of the deal they had with the shopkeepers and doormen of Santa Luzia Street. It was a verbal agreement without papers and signatures. As long as the

Angels didn't cause any trouble in Santa Luzia Street, they were allowed to sleep there at night. As soon as the first of the shutters were rolled up they had to scram.

Trouble could mean a lot of things. It meant robbing, breaking in, fighting, relieving themselves, and littering there. "You all do that somewhere else," the owner of the Deliro Tropical Bar had said.

The square was large and always busy. When the Angels had nothing to do, that was where they hung out. They weren't conspicuous there and you could always wangle something to eat. There were movie theaters, restaurants, and bars that were open until four in the morning, and there was a subway. At eleven at night the soup bus, as the Angels called it, would stop there. It was an old city bus with people who doled out soup to the homeless. Sometimes in the morning a VW van drove up from one of the streets with rolls and coffee, and there would be free breakfast.

It was noon and there was action in the air. In the square two posts were being set up. A beam was placed across the top. "Free Community-Sponsored Show" was written on a banner. A woman in a black leotard rolled a drop cloth out on the ground. Huff, Big Mouth, and Alex sat on a stone bench and watched.

"See those hips," said Big Mouth. "She's so hot! Oi-oi." He heaved a deep sigh.

The woman stuck her hands into a bowl of talc and had herself hoisted up toward the beam. People were on their lunch breaks. Around the tarp a large crowd of secretaries and office clerks who worked in the high-rises around the square had gathered.

"Cigarettes, cigarettes," cried a vendor. He had a wooden tray hanging in front of his stomach on which five packs of different kinds of cigarettes stood like soldiers standing at attention. A man with a briefcase bought a single cigarette. He leaned over for a light. His case was clamped under his arm.

Huff nudged Big Mouth. "Look at that briefcase." But Big Mouth had eyes only for the beautiful hips in the black leotard, now hanging ten feet above the ground and whizzing by, twirling.

Huff stomped hard on his foot.

"Ow, bastard!" exclaimed Big Mouth. "What you want?"

"Golden opportunity, boy. A case this big." Huff held his hands up three feet apart. "And you're sitting there snoozing. Well, now it's gone. Just ask Crusoe."

The audience clapped enthusiastically and Beautiful Hips jumped down. Big Mouth stamped his feet and yelled, "Bravo!" Out of the loudspeaker beside the tarp came the sound of violins. Two guys with painted faces walked onto the drop cloth.

"Aaww," said Big Mouth. There was a tone of disappointment in his voice. "I want an encore." He got up on the stone bench and shouted, "More! We want more!" Some of the people looked around at the black boy with the baseball cap who stood there clapping all by himself. The two guys on the tarp waved politely. They waved again. They wanted to start. But Big Mouth ignored their gestures.

"We want more!" he chanted from the bench.

Huff pulled at his shorts and yelled up, "You crazy, man? Somebody's going to call the juvenile court judge and they'll take you away. They'll say you were disturbing the peace."

Big Mouth, shaken by this, stepped down.

"Let's go chase up some scratch. Let's go have a good huff," said Huff, and he nodded at two women who had made their way out of the crowd and were walking in the direction of the subway. They both had shoulder bags.

"All right," said Big Mouth.

Alex watched the two of them as they disappeared among the other pedestrians.

"Nothing," sighed Huff when he got back fifteen minutes later and had sat down beside Alex again. "You can't do anything. It's crawling with cops."

"What about Big Mouth?" asked Alex.

"He's getting an autograph," replied Huff.

"An autograph?"

"Yeah, from Beautiful Hips," said Huff and he grinned broadly.

The missed lunch-break opportunities were eating at Huff.

It was about two hours later. They had played soccer with an empty can on an abandoned construction site behind the subway entrance. Huff lay sweating and trying to catch his breath, and Alex was using a straightened-out paper clip to try to fix one of his flip-flops, which had broken while he was playing soccer.

"I want to slam, Crusoe." That meant something like scoring good money or getting really high. By now Alex knew most of the street slang. "We're going to clean some cars. Come on."

Alex didn't really understand what Huff meant after all. There were carwashers who stood on the curb with cans of water, but they had chased him away when he had offered to be a water carrier for them. They were afraid that the customers would keep on driving if they saw street kids under the trees. Maybe Huff had befriended a carwasher, thought Alex.

Huff took an empty bottle out of a garbage can, smashed its neck off, and gave the jagged neck to Alex. "Here, you stick that in the face of that witch. Or you push it good on her wrist." Huff stretched out his arm, turned his wrist outward, and let the bottleneck rest on it. "See, like that, and then you give it a good push."

Alex looked at him, shocked. "What do you mean? We were

going to wash cars, weren't we?"

Huff snorted. "Cleaning is looting, stupid. Robbing, stealing, boosting. How long you been living on the street? It's a miracle you haven't starved to death yet."

Alex kept his mouth shut and stared at his newly repaired thong. He couldn't admit that he had never stolen before. Huff would laugh in his face.

"Look. See that Escort coming this way?"

Alex saw a red car with a man in it. He nodded.

"You go over to the window and say, 'Your wallet, make it fast. Or I'll cut you.' Then you show him the piece of glass. I'll wait for you over here."

Alex nodded. He felt the bottleneck in his right pocket. He made motions to go, but Huff grabbed his arm. "Another thing. You have to do it so that none of the other drivers notices anything. If there's one next to you with a gun in the glove compartment, you've had it." Alex swallowed.

God, what was he getting into? But he couldn't back out now. Slowly he walked over to the cars that were stopped at the light. The light turned green and off they went.

"Stupid. You got to be quick," said Huff when he was back on the sidewalk. "Look. Over there, the gray one." He shoved Alex out onto the pavement.

"And?" he asked when Alex got back.

"He had the windows closed and he didn't see me," said Alex. It wasn't a lie. The driver had looked straight ahead as if he knew that Alex was standing next to him. Alex had been grateful to him.

"Then you knock, idiot. So he opens the window." Huff looked at Alex with disdain.

A new line of cars presented itself at the intersection.

"Take that woman there, in the middle," Huff said, pointing.

Alex took a deep breath. This time he would force himself.

Her tanned arm was sticking halfway out of the open window. She was singing along with the radio and at first didn't hear what he was saying.

"Hand over your money or I'll cut you." Alex repeated the order, but louder this time.

She turned her head toward him. Alex saw big blue eyes.

"What did you say, boy?"

"Hand over your money," said Alex. On second thought, the bit about cutting was pretty crude.

"And if I don't have any money?" She smiled.

Alex didn't have a quick answer to that. "Uh then … uuhh … nothing," he said. Her eyes made him feel bashful. He hadn't known that such blue eyes existed, except in advertisements. "You're very pretty, ma'am," he blurted out.

"Thank you," she said and her eyes seemed even bluer. She tapped his arm. "Watch out, darling. The light's green." Then she waved and drove off.

Alex walked back to the curb. He felt a little drunk.

"And? And?" Huff grabbed him by the arms. "Was it a hit?"

"Uh …," said Alex.

"What? A hundred *real*?" Huff sounded surprised and excited at the same time.

"No," Alex began again. "She … didn't have any money."

"Yeah, they all say that. Then you have to push. Cut, man." Huff couldn't hide his impatience.

"But she really didn't have any money."

Huff glared at him and spat on the ground. "Chickenshit," he said and walked away.

The Dropout

Even though he belonged to Duda and Roy's group, Alex still felt like the original Crusoe: alone. After the adventure with Huff at the stoplights it had gotten worse. Duda was the only one who had taken his side. "Not everybody has as much courage as you do, Huff," she had said when Huff told his tale of woe.

Huff had snorted in disdain. "He's a chickenshit."

Alex knew deep down in his heart that Huff was right. It wasn't that he felt sorry for rich people; anybody driving a car had plenty of money. He simply didn't dare steal.

He was scared that somebody would shoot him. Or that he would be caught. He was scared that the police would beat him and kick him, like that one time at the samba stadium, or that he would end up in a home. But he was especially scared that he would miss his chance at adoption. Who's going to take in a thief? If he had a record he'd be doomed to stay on the street. When he thought of that, he panicked. He had no time to lose. How many days would he be able to last without stealing? The others didn't seem to worry about doing it. They saw stealing as work. Big Mouth even said whenever he went off thieving, "I got some work to do." Huff had proudly told him that in the ghetto where he had lived he was called Bloodhound. Alex didn't get it. He also didn't understand why the Angels didn't wash their clothes. Didn't they care how they looked? Did they want people to be scared and disgusted by them? He hated the street. They didn't.

The others felt he was different. They all played soccer together, but they didn't ask him to go into the city with them. When food was bought, they made fun of him. "Taste good, Crusoe? Worked hard too, huh?"

Whenever they had money, they gave him none of it. Sometimes he thought it was because of Duda that he was allowed to stay with the group. He was sure she stood up for him.

When the others talked about stealing, he pretended he was asleep. Often he would get up early and stroll through the city all day. When he was hungry, he drank water. If his stomach started growling, he went to a bakery and asked for day-old bread. They would give that away. Or else he would panhandle.

He often went to the pier. There he would sit and watch the tankers and fishing boats go by and the airplanes that swooped like big silver birds over the bay. He played with the stray cats, tossed stones into the water, and tried to catch fish with a thread the way he had learned from Robson. Robson, whom he had never seen again after they said good-bye and who probably sat down every day to a well-laid table and was able to cry his heart out on Vera's perfumed breast.

He felt different from the others, but nobody saw it. On the street people clutched their bags close when he walked by, as if they were scared that he would snatch them away. He wanted to yell loudly, I'm not what you think! But he didn't. Nobody would get it. They wouldn't believe it anyhow. Anybody who was poor and lived on the street was a thief. That was the way they thought. Because how else would he get money to eat?

When he returned in the afternoon, the others were often lying on the grass by the fountain sniffing glue. Every day Roy arranged for a can of glue. That, too, Alex only half understood. How could they take that stuff every single day? It stank like hell and made you as thick as a board. Some street kids sniffed acetone, the stuff you remove nail polish with. Other sniffers bought paint thinner. The Asphalt Angels took cobbler's glue. "It's good and strong," said Huff when Alex asked about it one time.

It was seven o'clock and there was a line of cars honking at the intersection. Roy had just opened a new can of glue and was doling it out. Huff was talking, all the while waving around the plastic bag he was holding in his right hand. "… And then I said, 'I'll slice up your face, man.' And then of course he came through …"

Alex was only half listening. He was starting to be familiar with Huff's tales of glory. He looked at the pinched-shut plastic bag. The glue stuck to the sides like greasy foam rubber. Now and then Huff interrupted his story and put the mouth of the bag to his mouth. He would inhale with his eyes closed.

Roy was being hassled from all sides. Scissors was hanging on his arm. "More, Roy. I want more."

"I want some in this Coke can," said Pear.

Big Mouth shoved Pear aside. "Me first."

"Jesus, *cara*, you always cut in front." Pear sank his teeth into Big Mouth's shoulder.

"Ow, fag! Stupid queer," screamed Big Mouth. And he gave Pear a jab with his elbow.

"He's bothering me, he's bothering me," Pear yelled, falling on the ground.

Alex was sitting on the grass. By now he was accustomed to arguments and punching. They're like animals, he thought. Once at school he had seen a film about the zoo. The lions, growling, had thrown themselves on the meat that was dumped into their cage. It was the same with the can of glue.

Duda gulped air greedily from her plastic bag. The beautiful Duda—her too. She grinned when she saw him looking and held out her bag to him. Her body leaned heavily against his.

"No," said Alex. "I already huffed." The sour smell stung his eyes and nose. He tried to breathe very carefully. He didn't want to get any of that stink inside. What if he became addicted? That he had already sniffed was a lie. He didn't want to go crazy and run out in the street like some wild man gone berserk. Then everybody would be able to use him and he wouldn't know anything anymore. "What happens for you, Duda?" Alex asked.

Smiling, she looked at him and lay her head on his shoulder. "Hmm, what?"

"Tell me what you see."

It was quiet. Duda sucked in her breath and shut her eyes. As if she were gone from the world for a moment. Slowly her eyes opened.

"I see the city move. The pavement's dancing. The buildings are bending over. Like they want to touch you. Everywhere there are little hearts in the sky. Oh Crusoe, Crusoe!" These last words she cried out as if she had been scared by something.

"What's wrong?"

"The water in the fountain just turned red. It looks just like blood."

Alex turned around. Clear water was squirting out of the fountain as usual. Duda was crazy.

"Oh Crusoe, now the blood is squirting back. It's running into the ground. And now it's coming back out again. Crusoe, it's got cars in it."

Alex didn't know what he should do. Roy was sitting on the rim of the fountain with his back to them, talking with a man. Alex put his hand on Duda's forehead and stroked it. Very slowly, because you never knew what she was seeing and whether she might go for his throat the next minute. She didn't. She looked at him bleary-eyed and then rolled onto her side.

Alex lay down. His new pals were high. Duda was seeing little hearts and flying cars, and when he sniffed glue Scissors talked with the lions. For Big Mouth the buildings were rocking and rolling. Alex was scared but he didn't know of what.

He looked up. The night was black and the stars were not little hearts but simply white pinpoints. Then he saw a boy. You almost couldn't make him out because he was just as black as the night. Even his teeth were black. He sat motionless on a big, empty lawn.

The next day he went to the beach.

"Where have you been? I've missed you," said Dona Lica when he plopped down in the sand beside her bar.

"I moved." You could call it that, he thought.

"I'll be. And where are you living now?" she asked.

"In Copacabana." It was out before he had thought twice.

"Weell . . . " she said, looking at him searchingly. "Do you have a new mother? Have you been adopted?"

"Yes." Now that he had lied, there was no turning back. Besides, he couldn't say that he slept on a piece of cardboard every night with glue sniffers and street thieves.

"Geez, you lucked out," she said. "Just be thankful. She must be a very special woman, that foster mother of yours. Don't get me wrong. But who wants a boy who's thirteen and black? Nobody. Child, people who adopt want a baby. And then preferably one that's white and has blond hair and blue eyes."

"What about Robson?" Alex asked.

"My boy Robson … Robson had a lot of luck. Just like you. And don't forget: he's a nice-looking boy. Nice white teeth. Cute smile. Polite."

Alex was silent. He thought of his teeth. So did she mean that he was impolite and didn't have a cute smile?

Dona Lica noticed nothing; she just went on talking. "Robson comes by now and again. Usually with that girl, his new sister I should say. He's doing very well."

Alex felt a pang of jealousy. Couldn't he ask Robson … ? No, the apartment was small. He shouldn't mess up Robson's chances. And Dona Lica was right. Who wanted a black boy with rotten teeth?

Dona Lica rattled on. She talked about Luís the guard, who now had a baby. And the two girls who'd been run over by a beer truck when they were crossing the highway. And Zé Carlos, the unemployed engineer who had sold coconuts next to her on the beach for four years and disappeared overnight. "One day he's there as if he's always been there. Then suddenly he's gone and you'll never know why."

Alex nodded. He was hungry, but he was scared that Dona Lica would grill him about his nonexistent new mother. So he said good-bye and walked into the streets of the neighborhood near the beach.

He went into the bakery overlooking the park. People with receipts in their hands were standing in line along the glass display case filled with sweet rolls.

"And?" the baker's assistant in a blue uniform asked. He tapped impatiently on the glass counter.

"Would you have some coffee for me?" asked Alex. He handed the plastic cup he had found in the trash over the counter. The boy looked at his boss, who was sitting in a cubicle with the cash register. Then he quickly filled the cup and cocked his head to the side. As if to say, And now, be gone.

On the stoop in front of the bakery Alex slurped down the coffee. He could hear the basket of fresh rolls being dumped out onto the shelves. The sweet aroma wrapped around him like a blanket. How he wanted a fresh roll! The kind with the crust that would shatter when you sank your teeth into it.

Out of the corner of his eye he took stock of the man behind the cash register. A goon, Robson would say. If Alex was careful, maybe the man wouldn't notice anything. Alex slipped beside a woman in a flowered dress at the tail end of the line.

"Uh, ma'am." She paid no attention. He tugged at her skirt. "Would you have some money for me? I'm so hungry."

She stared at him and kept staring at him. Her gaze ran from his flip-flops with the wire up to his nappy hair and back down again. Come on, lady, thought Alex. Either you hand it over or you don't.

It was as if she had read his thoughts. "No," she said. "You'll buy glue with it anyway."

"But I don't sniff glue," he said defiantly. "And if you don't believe me, buy me something instead. A sweet roll is fine too." Because he really wanted one of those, he decided.

"Gee, the gentleman has wishes, too," said the woman, pointedly turning her head the other way.

Stingy bitch, thought Alex. Cheapskate. What was eight *centavos* anyway? That was all a roll cost.

The bald head was still bent over the cash register. Anyhow,

Alex's hunger was greater than his fear.

Number two was an old man in shorts with a newspaper under his arm. He jumped as Alex spoke.

"No, no. I don't have anything," he said.

Jesus, thought Alex.

The little metal door by the cash register flapped. "Leave my customers alone."

Alex looked up and saw the boss coming toward him. His head was red and shiny.

"What are you standing there gawking for? Didn't you hear me? Beat it." He stood with legs planted and his hands on his hips.

Alex swallowed. He wanted to say something back, but only air came out of his mouth. Everybody in line was staring at him. The assistant behind the counter stepped closer. The woman in the flowered dress squared her shoulders.

"Freeloader," said the boss. "You should be ashamed of yourself, a young boy like you. Go work instead of holding out your hand."

A lightning bolt shot through Alex's spine. "Then give me a job. But you won't, will you!" The woman in the dress exchanged glances with the man next to her. "You ... you ..." Alex stammered in anger. He didn't care anymore what they thought of him. "You're all big fat pigs! You're rich and keep everything for yourselves. You all have houses and eat three times a day. But eight *centavos* for a roll, you won't give that away."

Everybody stared, but nobody said anything. The checkout man took a step in his direction. "Now get going. And don't you ever dare come back here again."

Alex walked back slowly. In his head there was churning and rattling. Near the television building, a group of men stood talking. They stopped when he came by. Farther up a doorman in uniform was sweeping the sidewalk. Was he imagining it, or had he really stepped back as Alex passed? Again he felt rage rise up inside. What did they know about him? They could all take a hike.

In Gloria Square near the subway entrance sat three street kids with their plastic bags in their hands. He reckoned they were just as old as he was. Two others were sliding on the handrail of the steps that led down. They were barefoot and wore T-shirts as if they were dresses.

In front of the display window of a shoe store at the next corner Alex stood still. In the glass he could see himself. At first he was shocked. He had gotten skinnier and his hair was a rat's nest. But the rest of him looked normal, he decided.

In the square he saw only Big Mouth and Pear. Duda had gone to her mother's, Big Mouth told him. She had run into a neighbor girl who had told her her mother was sick. Huff and Roy had gone to take care of a little business. Scissors was watching television. The children's programs with cartoons were on in the morning.

Pear was bending over a tiny pocket mirror popping zits.

"Are you coming?" Big Mouth said to Pear.

"Wait a minute, *cara*," mumbled Pear. "Ow … wait … yeah … yeah. Aha, there it goes." Pear glanced up from the mirror. "Hey, hello there, Crusoe." And then to Big Mouth, "Look at what a fat one." He held the mirror up like a silver platter.

Big Mouth looked at the results of all the hard work. "It looks just like a worm. You had a worm in your cheek, Pear. Yuck."

"Where are you guys going?" asked Alex. He was seeing double with hunger and was hoping that his street pals would offer some solution.

"We're going to Bob's," said Big Mouth. Alex knew Bob's. It

was a hamburger joint on the corner of a wide street. Outside the Angels' turf but on neutral terrain. There weren't any Germans there, as the Angels called other gangs.

"I'm coming," said Alex. Big Mouth and Pear looked at each other. That wasn't the Alex they knew.

The Briefcase

Bob's was crowded because it was close to noon. You could sit indoors or outdoors. From a loudspeaker a voice called numbers.

They were standing outside on the sidewalk.

"Now where is that guy?" Big Mouth scouted around.

"Who?" asked Alex.

"The bouncer," replied Big Mouth. "He's straight. He usually gives us a bag of fries if we promise not to hang around. He doesn't want any street kids at the door."

"What does he look like?" Alex wanted to know. A bag of fries: it was music to his ears.

"Big guy, black hair and a mustache. He usually wears a Hawaiian shirt."

There was no big man with a Hawaiian shirt. Hamburgers on trays kept coming by. The aroma of food made Alex feel faint.

"Crusoe." Big Mouth stood behind him and was whispering to him. "Crusoe, see that man sitting over there? To the left."

Alex looked. At a small table on the sidewalk sat a man wearing light-colored pants, talking with a young woman. Beside him on the seat stood a briefcase.

"Pear will distract him and you jack his briefcase. They don't know you. We'll meet back at the fountain."

Big Mouth gave him a shove. Alex jumped. He was as hungry as a horse, but he hadn't yet thought of stealing. Out of the corner of his eye Alex saw that Pear, who had been sitting on the edge of the stoop, was getting up. He felt light-headed, but he didn't know whether it was because he hadn't eaten or from nerves. When Pear started talking to him, the man would turn away from his briefcase. Then Alex had to grab it. If he didn't pull it off this time, the Angels would surely kick him out of the group.

Alex calculated the distance between himself and the table. Five steps.

Ai, the man was looking at Pear now. Alex carefully stepped forward while he kept the table in sight out of the corner of his eye. His legs were shaking.

"Sir. I saw you on television. It was you, wasn't it? Can I have your autograph?" Pear's high voice you could always hear above everything. What a line, thought Alex. You could count on Pear.

"No," said the man. "I wasn't on television. You're …"

Alex was almost at the table. Carefully he reached out his hand toward the briefcase. He hoped nobody was looking.

The man smiled. If only he didn't look around now.

Got it. Alex clutched the briefcase close as if to make it invisible and sneaked away. Three steps slowly and now run.

"Stop the thief! Stop the thief!" Behind him he heard shouts and the sound of folding chairs knocked over.

He hugged the briefcase tighter and ran straight through the moving cars. Out of sight, he had to get out of sight. Where was a side street? Alex ran so fast that he didn't feel his toes getting scraped on the pavement. He was panting; his heart seemed to be hanging in his throat. He didn't dare look back. Or take off his flip-flops.

Only after he had rounded three corners did he stop. He was standing in a street with lots of garages. There was nobody around. His head pounded and he had to steady himself on the wall, his legs were shaking so badly. He put the briefcase down on the ground.

Only now did he have a chance to look at it closely. It was made of brown leather and had shiny gold locks on it. He couldn't walk across the square that way. A street kid with a diplomat's case. He saw himself walking past the police box. He wouldn't outlive that. Alex looked around. He had to wrap the briefcase up, in a plastic bag, for instance. The only thing he could find was a crumpled newspaper.

That was how he walked across the square: with a big package wrapped in a newspaper. He had even found a strip of plastic to tie it all together. He was relieved. Now the stolen briefcase was Big Mouth's problem. Alex had done what he had to and he didn't want to have anything more to do with it. What had that blowhard done up till now anyway? Nothing, right?

Big Mouth was sitting by the fountain as planned. He had a half-eaten roll of cookies in his hand. He looked startled when Alex came up. "Crusoe, where's the briefcase?"

Alex set the package down on the grass and stuck his hand out for the cookies. He was seeing double from hunger.

"The briefcase, man. Cat got your tongue?"

"If fanding vare." Alex had just popped three cookies into his mouth at the same time and was spraying crumbs.

"I already washed this morning, thank you very much," said Big Mouth as he wiped the spatters from his cheek. "Talk normal, man. I knew it. Out with it. You lost the thing, right?"

"It's standing there." Alex took a deep breath and shoved another three cookies into his mouth. How hungry he was.

"Where?" Big Mouth jumped up.

"Vare." Alex nodded in the direction of the package as he chewed.

Big Mouth tore off the paper and tried to open the snaps. "Jesus, it's locked." Out of his pocket he pulled a piece of wire and started fiddling.

Alex had polished off the cookies and was able to think again. "Hey, where's Pear?"

"Ai, damn briefcase. Come on, pal. Open up the gate." Big Mouth was completely preoccupied in his battle with the briefcase.

"Heeyy," shouted Alex in Big Mouth's ear. "What about Pear?"

Disturbed, Big Mouth looked up. "Be here in a minute. Ran into a friend on the way."

Alex lay down and thought about food. The cookies had made him even more hungry. He felt like a plate of steaming black beans with bits of orange. And fries. Crispy, golden fries. Or mashed potatoes the way his mother made them. So thick that your spoon could stand up in them.

"Hi, ace." Pear stood over them, one hand seductively on his hip. Lying on the ground Alex could easily look up into the cut-off legs of his shorts. But he couldn't see anything. Pear was black and it was black inside there too.

"Damn briefcase," growled Big Mouth. He still hadn't gotten it open.

"Let's go see Captain," said Pear. "He'll have it open in two seconds."

Big Mouth brightened up right away.

"Who's Captain?" asked Alex, sitting up.

"Don't you know him? You're from the Central Station, aren't you?" Pear looked at him questioningly.

Alex didn't respond.

"He's the most famous car thief of the Central. He can open anything. He used to be a sailor. That's why they call him Captain."

"But what about the Platform Panthers?" said Big Mouth. "I don't need that scene right now." The Central Station and the square in front of it were enemy territory. Alex remembered Duda had told him that the first day.

Pear considered. "What time is it? Two o'clock? If you ask me they'll be lying out on the beach now. Besides, Captain is usually at the pool hall on the corner in the afternoon. If we do it right, the Panthers won't see us."

It was just as Pear had said. There was no sign of the Panthers anywhere, and Captain was in the bar playing pool. He was broad-shouldered and had white hair. Out of his pocket he pulled an enormous keyring with all sorts of little knives and pins and, of course, keys. He selected a little key and carefully moved it back and forth in the little lock. Captain had his eyes shut. After that he picked out a little pin. And—*boing*—the lock popped open.

"There you are, gentlemen. It is not, I trust, a stolen briefcase, hm?" He gave Alex an exaggerated wink.

Alex didn't know where to look. Had the guy figured it out?

As they were leaving, Captain grabbed Pear's arm. "Hey, honey. Running off just like that. Aren't you going to give me a kiss?"

The men in the barroom laughed.

"Let go of me, *cara*. Heellp!" cried Pear. Alex looked for Big

Mouth. He was standing outside and acted as if he hadn't heard anything. He had wrapped the briefcase back up in the newspaper.

Abashed, Alex walked out too. Pear would just have to get out of this by himself. Alex wasn't some Karate Kid.

Inside there was more laughter and then out came Pear, still muttering but also looking a little bit proud. He ran his fingers through his hair. "Does it look all right?"

"Sure." Big Mouth was in a hurry now that the prize was within reach. He pulled Pear along.

In a little back street they sat down behind a parked car. The briefcase lay on the pavement. Solemnly Big Mouth clicked the snaps open.

"Holy shit," cried Pear. He rifled through the papers, reports, and receipts.

"Easy there," said Big Mouth, who looked as if he'd won the lottery. In a side compartment Pear found a wallet with photos, credit cards, and money. Quickly he counted. "Yahoo! Forty-three *real.*"

Big Mouth was disappointed. "Forty-three *real?*"

Alex studied the wallet. There was a photo in it of two smiling children. A father who carried around a picture of his kids. How he wanted a father like that too. What would the man tell his kids tonight? It was a boy just like you? He bit his lip. For the first time he felt regret.

"Hey, look." Big Mouth held a little doll in his hand. It was a cloth doll the size of a finger.

Pear looked scared. "That's Exu, the devil. Uh-oh, now we've had it." He threw his hands over his face.

"Aw, it's not like that," said Big Mouth. "It brings good luck. Except not to him, to us. He lost his briefcase, didn't he? So the devil didn't help him. But he did help us because we have a briefcase and forty *real*." He brought the doll up to his lips.

Alex recalled the figurine in the bedroom at home. His step-father regularly called on the devil's help. Suddenly he flashed on what the neighbor boy had said right before he left Japeri. His stepfather had made a big sacrifice to the devil. You do that only if you want the devil to kill somebody, the neighbor boy had said.

What do you do when you never have anything and suddenly you're forty *real* rich? That was a problem. The whole way back Pear, Alex, and Big Mouth argued about it. Pear wanted to buy glue and kicks; Alex wanted kicks. Big Mouth wanted a nylon baseball jacket embroidered on the back, because he already had kicks and a cap.

No matter what, they couldn't go to the square. If they ran into Huff and Roy, they'd have to share. So they decided to go to Copacabana.

The briefcase was thrown into an empty dumpster. Big Mouth split the money between himself and Pear. If one of the two was nabbed by the police, the other in any case still had twenty *real*. He had slipped the devil doll gently into his pocket.

"But I'm not going with my kicks on," said Big Mouth. "Those Germans in Copa are bad. They'll take your kicks away from you in no time." Pear thought he was absolutely right.

"They buy dope with them," Pear explained to Alex. "A lit-tle packet of coke for a pair of kicks." It made Alex grin. They stole too, didn't they?

Big Mouth whipped the cover off the manhole in Santa Luzia Street, took out his flip-flops, and hid his sneakers under a news-paper in the hole. He thought for a second and then took the doll out of his pocket. He laid it on top of the newspaper. Clearly visible. "If anybody sees this, he'll be out of here real quick," he reassured Alex.

A boy walked up.

"Hey, where are you guys going?" he asked. He looked a little cross-eyed.

Big Mouth turned around. "Oh, it's you." His voice sounded irritated. "It doesn't matter where we're going, because you aren't coming anyway."

"Why not?" asked the boy. Alex didn't know him. He was barefoot and wore shorts. Alex figured he was fifteen. He had bleached his dark hair.

"Lerdo, quit whining. We've got business to take care of. Just us, get it?"

"And you're going to do that with flip-flops on. You can't run with no flip-flops," the boy insisted.

"Well, we wear flip-flops. Now beat it."

"I want to go too."

"Beat it!"

The boy turned around and walked away. After two steps he stopped. "I'll get you for this, blabbermouth," he yelled loudly.

"Who's Lerdo?" asked Alex when they were on the bus. Because they didn't want to get into trouble with the driver and had money anyway, they had gone through the turnstile.

Big Mouth explained. Lerdo, Slow, wanted to be with the Angels, but he hadn't been voted in. So now he drifted. "He's just bad news. A little bit like you, Crusoe." Big Mouth gave him a fake smile. He paused for a few seconds to measure the effect. "No, not really, Crusoe, that was a joke. Today you were hitting, man. Slow is real bad. He's dumb and retarded at the same time, see. He bugs, know what I mean? Because he huffed too much glue when he was little."

Alex nodded but said nothing. How could Big Mouth say something like that about huffing glue and be sucking on a plastic bag every day himself? He didn't understand that.

Copacabana

Alex had been in Copacabana once with his mother and also one time with Robson. Each time it had been exciting. In Copacabana he felt like an ant walking through a forest of apartment buildings. When you looked up you saw a thin strip of blue sky. Down on the street, life was busy and full. You couldn't just walk down the sidewalk. Underpants, plastic flowers, sugar-coated peanuts, teddy bears, windshield wipers, Nintendo games. The craziest thing you could think of and they were selling it on the sidewalks of Copacabana. There were vendors hawking everywhere.

You didn't have just one or two buses driving behind another one, but a hundred. You could forget crossing the street quickly in Copacabana. Whenever the lights turned green, six lanes of cars would come roaring up.

The finest thing of all, Alex thought, was the sea. When you went to Copacabana, you had to go through a tunnel. As soon as the bus came out of the tunnel you could see the sea with its whitecaps. Before it lay the most beautiful beach Alex had ever seen. It was big and white. From the sidewalk you couldn't see what was happening at the surfline, the beach was so wide. Like the sidewalks, it was always crowded.

"I want a banana slit with whipped cream," said Pear. They were standing at the top of the esplanade.

Alex, who was looking at a group of volleyball players, turned around right away. In all the excitement he had forgotten that he was hungry. "That's fly, yeah, I want one too!"

"It's a banana s*p*lit," said Big Mouth, stressing the p.

On the terrace with parasols like mushrooms they ate their banana splits, and after that they lay on the beach. After five minutes Pear had fallen asleep. Big Mouth lay on his stomach so he could see all the girls sway by on the beach. Alex looked through the slits of his eyes at the blue sky. The stealing had been a lot easier than he had imagined. That man shouldn't have been so dumb. Who would put a briefcase down next to himself like that? If Alex hadn't grabbed it, another boy would have.

He thought of his mother. If she were still alive, he wouldn't have dared tell her. But maybe she had seen it. From heaven you could see everything, of course. The idea gave Alex a fright. He opened his eyes wide. Nothing in the blue expanse suggested his mother's presence. Strange, but he had the feeling that she was closer to him at night. During the day with all the noise and people she was probably busy with other things. But he would be able to explain himself to her if she were to say anything about it. If nobody gave him anything, he had to steal. Otherwise he'd starve to death. That's what he would say.

Big Mouth was growing restless. He had gotten up a couple of times.

"Let's go down the esplanade," he said to Alex. With his right foot he gave Pear a nudge in the ribs.

"Wh ... what?" Pear bolted up.

"This is a holdup. Hand over your money or I'll slice up your face," Big Mouth joked.

"Stupid jerk," said Pear indignantly. He shook the sand out of his shorts and grabbed his flip-flops.

It was getting to be evening. The esplanade sidewalk was slowly filling up with joggers, cyclists, and walkers. Parents with children, big and little, were also out walking. Amazing that they had the time to go out and take a walk with their children, thought Alex. He had seen his mother only on Sundays, when she didn't have to work.

"Downtown's a good place to live, but Copa's good for boosting," said Big Mouth as they walked along with the crowd. "I know this guy and he makes two hundred *real* a day. Just with a piece of glass."

"Two hundred *real*?" Alex repeated.

"This is where the flow is, *cara*. The place is just packed with foreigners, see. And they got dollars. Dollars are worth a lot more than *real*."

"That's not true," said Pear. "You get less if you pay with a dollar."

Big Mouth was thrown off for a minute by the sudden contradiction. "But you can buy a lot more with it," he finally said.

"Naw, like what?" Pear challenged him.

"Like those basketball sneakers. All the tourists wear those. And they all have dollars."

Pear had nothing to say to that. He was quiet for a moment. "They say foreigners aren't scared of handguns." It was something he had heard on the street and that had really surprised him. "You put the blaster in their face and they don't give you their money. They think you're joking, because a kid can't have a gun and shooting is movie stuff."

"Then they should come on down here. I know this guy who's fifteen and he walks around with an AR15," said Big Mouth.

"An AR15? What's that?" asked Alex.

"It's an automatic rifle. This big." Big Mouth held his arms way far apart. "It sounds like rat-tat-tat-tat-rat-tat-tat. The guy's a banger for some dealer."

"Oh." Alex thought everything having to do with drugs was scary. Did Big Mouth have something to do with drugs too? he wondered.

"They are scared of knives," Pear continued.

"Look, there's two over there." Big Mouth pointed at two men in shorts walking in front of them. Their legs were as white as candles.

Big Mouth, Alex, and Pear quickened their pace.

"They're pretty big," said Alex. "Are all foreigners that big?"

"Yeah, because they eat better over there." Pear was sure.

"But they got real white legs."

"That's because they drink lots of milk."

"C'mon, Pear," said Big Mouth. "You're the best-looking of the three of us. Go on over there and ask them for some money."

Pear stuck out his tongue and walked up behind them, swinging his hips. "Hello."

The two men didn't hear him.

"Helloooohooo." Pear said it again, but a lot louder this time. The two turned around.

Encouraged by this success, Pear continued. "Monnie, monnie." He poked his stomach with his index finger. "Hunker. Hunker."

The men talked between themselves. One of them felt around in his pocket and gave Pear a bill. Pear made a little bow and ran back.

"Look."

Big Mouth and Alex couldn't believe their eyes. Pear had scored two *real*.

"Fresh," said Alex.

"A Brazilian would never give that much," Big Mouth declared.

"Brazilians abuse kids," said Pear. "I don't want to have anything to do with anybody except foreigners." He blew the two walking candles a kiss.

"They're high rollers. Did you know that everybody over there's got a house and a swimming pool?" said Big Mouth. He'd seen that in a movie. "There aren't any buses over there at all, because everybody's got a car."

"But they weren't wearing basketball sneakers," said Alex.

"That's right," Pear agreed. "They were wearing flip-flops, just like us."

"These two were poor high rollers," said Big Mouth.

Alex only half believed this, but Big Mouth knew more about the world than he did. So he kept his mouth shut.

He looked down the esplanade. A girl sitting on a parked car waved at him. She was wearing hot pants and a black lace top.

"You know her?" asked Big Mouth.

"Noooo." Alex knew for sure he didn't. He was a stranger in the city. Besides, he didn't know any white girls with black hair down to their waists. You had hardly any of those in Japeri.

"If you ask me, she's looking at you," said Pear to Big Mouth.

"Shhh. Fag, shut your mouth." Big Mouth straightened his back and walked over to the car.

"Hi there."

"Hi." The girl smiled.

Pear and Alex nudged each other. Big Mouth always scored with the ladies.

"You waiting for somebody?" asked Big Mouth.

"You," she said and smiled again.

"Me?" repeated Big Mouth. He sounded surprised. Then he turned to Pear and Alex. "Hey, you guys, you go on and sit for a while, over there on that bench. Looks like I'll be busy for a while."

From the bench Alex and Pear watched Big Mouth sit down on the car beside the girl. He made her laugh a lot and she shook her hair. Now and then she'd lean up against him. After a couple of minutes he threw his arm around her.

"Goal," said Pear. "He sure got her going."

Not much later Big Mouth came walking up. "Listen. We're going to go … get something … to drink. We'll meet you back here in an hour."

"Hmmm, something to drink. He's acting like he thinks we're retards or something," said Alex. He watched the two until they disappeared around the corner.

"Damn, he's got the money on him." Pear slapped his forehead. "We can forget those twenty *real*."

"What do you mean?" asked Alex.

"You think it don't cost anything? A ho in Copa, that's laying it out. Look." Pear pointed down the esplanade. "You think they live on air?"

Now Alex saw. There were girls sitting on almost all the cars. He thought Big Mouth was just plain stupid. Alex would never pay for a girl. You could just go with another one. Plenty of them.

Pear was counting the money. They had seven *real*. "Let's go get something to eat," he said. That seemed like a good idea to Alex.

Over an hour later Big Mouth came back. He was by himself.

"Well?"

"Totally dope, man. What a piece, man." He stuck his thumb up. He had put his baseball cap on backwards. He did that when he was in a good mood.

"So, and?" With his thumb and forefinger Pear made a sign meaning money.

"Tight," said Big Mouth.

"What do you mean, tight? How much you still got?"

"Hey man, you know, she's got a kid. You got to be real … She asked me for some grip to buy food for the kid. And some clothes. I gave her that. I can't say no, can I?" Alex had never seen Big Mouth so at a loss for words.

"You didn't give her all of it, did you?" Pear's voice cracked.

"Uuhh, yeah," said Big Mouth.

"Man, you're out of your mind," said Pear. "And what about your friends?" He put a doleful look on his face. Pear was laying it on, Alex could tell by the glint in his eye.

They took the bus back and hung around the back seat because they didn't have any more money for tickets. Big Mouth drummed the seat and rapped in a low voice.

> *Just wanna feel fine*
> *Walkin' down the line,*
> *Down in the ghetto where I was born*
> *And I wanna feel proud:*
> *That even when you're broke*
> *you got a place to call your own.*

Alex stuck his head out of the open window. The wind blew through his hair. The bus made its way along the park. The band shell was an island of light in a park that was completely dark. On the floor lay two figures curled up under a white rag.

The Shoes

What do you feel like after a night lying on a piece of cardboard on hard stones? Like a leather football that's been in the washing machine for an hour: empty, stiff, and done for. Alex woke up at five-thirty. It was almost light out on the street. His right leg was asleep, his neck was stiff, and his head felt like a cavern. He was thirsty and had to pee.

At the entrance to the subway station he begged for money. He drank some water and ate a hot dog in the square, walked through the city, and looked at the water from the rocks. He would probably have forgotten this day later on if Big Mouth's sneakers had simply been in the manhole. But they weren't.

When he walked back, he heard the shouting from way off. "Where are my sneakers? Who's got my blasted kicks?"

"But you're sure that you put them there?" asked Huff, who

had been on the move all day.

"Course I am," growled Big Mouth. "I'll kill him. I'll kill him!"

"The question is who you have to kill," said Roy.

"Now you have to go to the house party wearing flip-flops, huh?" Scissors sympathized.

"Somebody knew those sneakers were in there. That you didn't have them on, I mean." Huff was trying to help.

Big Mouth, who had been pacing back and forth, jerked to a halt. "Slow. Slow saw. Where's Slow?"

At first nobody knew where Slow lived. According to Huff, he slept at the Central Station. "On top of a kiosk that sells newspapers."

"On top of the subway roof, you mean," cried Scissors. Scissors' favorite television store was right by the subway there. He knew all the local street vendors and street people.

Alex had occasionally seen that people slept on the slanting roof over the hole of the subway entrance. Clever, he thought. Nobody could see you and you had time to get away if they tried to climb up.

Scissors was right. He went to check it out with Huff and Roy. The two boys came back with Slow in between them and Scissors dancing around the threesome.

Big Mouth, who on Roy's orders had stayed in Santa Luzia Street, grabbed Slow by the arm. "Give me my kicks back, bastard."

Roy gave him a kick. "Sit down, *cara*. Leave this to me."

Reluctantly Big Mouth did as he was told.

Roy took Slow in a stranglehold. His arm was clamped around Slow's neck.

"Where are those sneakers?" asked Roy.

"What sneakers? I don't know nothing about no sneakers. I

never wear sneakers." Slow sounded as if he might burst into tears at any moment.

Alex looked down. Slow had feet that looked like wads of dough rolled flat. They were feet that had never worn shoes.

"Big Mouth had kicks. He can't find them and he thinks you stole them."

"I didn't."

"You did." Big Mouth took a piece of glass out of his bag and placed it on Slow's chest. "So talk."

Slow hiccuped. "Nuuuhhhuuuh."

Big Mouth gave him a kick. And another one.

"And now hit him," Scissors hooted.

Roy let Slow go. He motioned to Big Mouth to chill. "You aren't rid of us yet, boy. If I find out that you do have those shoes, you're dead. You can book. But as a punishment you've gotta go in your underwear."

Whoa, that Roy. You didn't play games with him, thought Alex.

Scissors clapped. "Yeah, yeah. In his underwear."

Slow didn't move a muscle.

"Didn't you hear me?"

"I don't got no underwear." He was quietly crying now.

Punk, thought Alex. Just like a girl.

"Then you'll just have to go bare-assed in the street," cried Big Mouth as he pulled Slow's shorts off.

Slow glared at him and then ran down the street in the direction of the Central Station.

"Bare ass dead ass bare ass dead ass," called Scissors, running a few steps after him.

"Tomorrow I'll go over to Central. If I find my kicks, I'll kill him," threatened Big Mouth.

Did he really mean it? Alex wondered. He looked at Big

Mouth. It would be easier to believe if it were Huff talking.

"Maybe he sold them to buy food," said Roy.

"Or swapped them," shouted Scissors. He looked at Huff, who gave him a kick. Did Huff know something about the sneakers? Alex wondered.

Pear, who came walking up late that evening, was alarmed when he heard the news about the stolen sneakers. "Big Mouth shouldn't ever have touched that doll. It's going to bring us bad luck. This is the punishment of the devil."

The night was a restless one. Scissors, who had sniffed glue all night, had to vomit. His skinny body shook. Roy gave him water, but even that he spit up.

In the restaurant at the end of the street the Friday night disco was hopping. Music blared in the arcade until four o'clock in the morning. There was the constant sound of footsteps, voices, and cars stopping at the curb.

At one point Alex saw two men who were spying on them from behind a parked car. His body grew alert. He felt to see if the broken bottleneck was still lying beside him. Then the men walked on. Alex didn't succeed in getting any more sleep. He had a scary feeling of foreboding. If the devil was against them, this was the beginning of the end.

But the next morning nothing happened that seemed like the beginning of the end. In the morning a van was parked at the corner of the square. It was from some church, Roy said. There were three girls inside who handed out coffee and bread to everybody. Alex ate two rolls, one with cheese and one with sausage. He couldn't remember the last time he had eaten so much in the morning.

That afternoon Big Mouth asked Alex to go with him and Pear. They walked through busy shopping streets where vendors stood shoulder to shoulder. They looked at cassettes and sneakers and hung for at least an hour in the pinball arcade, where they stared their eyes out at the supersonic bomber that could vaporize all the enemies on the screen with blue flashes of light.

In Ouvidor Street, narrow, high-walled, and crowded, Big Mouth stole a lady's purse as she stood talking. Alex hadn't seen a thing. Pear had to laugh. "You're fronting, you mean you really didn't see anything?"

There were ten *real* in the purse.

"You work and work and you still got nothing," said Big Mouth. "Nobody has money on them when they're out on the street. There's too many thieves."

"Old men are the best," said Pear. "They wear pants with deep pockets where they keep their money."

Toward eight, when the streets grew quiet, Pear saw a young man. He was wearing sports shoes you didn't usually see in Brazil, so he had to be rich. He was sitting on a post. He was waiting for his girlfriend, thought Alex.

Alex and Big Mouth were going to stand beside him so he couldn't get away and Pear was going to empty his pockets.

It was easier than Alex had thought. Big Mouth put his right hand under his T-shirt and poked his forefinger forward. "Hand over your money or you're dead," he said when they were standing beside the man.

The man was startled but he didn't move, not even when Pear bent down and felt inside his pockets. After that they ran away. Pear had two ten-*real* bills and one five. The checkbook he had taken for good measure, Big Mouth threw away. "That only brings trouble." With the twenty-five *real* they bought a bottle of Coke, chicken and rice, and glue.

While the others were lying around sniffing, Alex reflected. He had done hardly anything. He had only stood on the sidelines. Was he a thief too, then? The briefcase he had taken because the man hadn't paid attention well enough. Was that stealing? Maybe the man had kind of forgotten about it. Then it was finding something.

If this was stealing, it was easy, thought Alex. In any case easier than selling cookies. But he would only do it when it was almost dark and people couldn't see him well. What Huff did at the stoplights in broad daylight he thought was scary. What if one of the people in the car had a weapon?

The Packet

A couple of days later Roy called him over. "Crusoe, I need to talk to you for a minute."

Alex had noticed that everybody had treated him better since he had stolen the briefcase. Now and then he went "out working," as they called it, with Huff, Big Mouth, and Pear. Right away he was more a part of the crew, even though he didn't sniff glue.

"Crusoe, you want to slam?" asked Roy.

Alex's heart skipped a beat. He felt clammy. Roy never talked specially to him. What was he supposed to say? What did Roy want of him? He didn't want to get involved in any dirty dealings.

"What is it, man?" he said finally.

"There's a packet that's got to be picked up," said Roy. "You know the Morro da Providencia?"

Alex nodded. Everybody who lived downtown knew the Morro da Providencia. It was a ghetto on a hill right near the Central Station. On the top there was a big cross and they said it was the oldest ghetto in the city. It was located practically next to the prison. Sometimes when cons escaped, they would run to the Morro da Providencia. The police didn't dare go there. One time Alex had seen a military police chopper circling the hill. "Give yourselves up," they had shouted down through megaphones. The drug lord's men—you had those there too—had shot at the chopper. After that it had flown away.

"That's where you got to pick up a packet," said Roy.

Alex nodded. What else could he do? Feverishly he tried to think of a way out. If he refused, he'd be on his own again. Roy would toss him out of the group.

"You'll get thirty *real*," Roy continued.

Alex continued to keep his mouth shut.

Roy took it for consent. He started to explain which way Alex had to walk, what the guy who was going to give him a knapsack looked like, and where he had to go after that. Alex nodded and swallowed. He had no choice. He promised himself that this would be the first and last time.

In order to get to the hill Alex had to cross through enemy territory. On the square in front of the station the Platform Panthers were hanging out. What the argument with the Asphalt Angels was about, nobody knew. But it had started with soccer. The Angels had been for Flamengo and the Platform Panthers for Botafogo, another of Rio's soccer teams. Once the Angels had beaten up one of the Platform Panthers when he swore at them. After that the Panthers had taken revenge and pelted them with rocks on the square.

"Better for you to walk around than cross the square. The

Panthers don't know you, but you can't ever be too sure," Roy had said. He was fretting like an old thief that Alex would lose his precious load.

Alex walked as fast as his legs could carry him. The ghetto had two entrances, a switchback road for cars on the station side and a long stone staircase on the other side for pedestrians. The staircase was where he had to go, Roy had said.

He found it without any problem. The stairs were narrow and over a hundred steps long. On both sides there were houses. This made the stairs look more like a steep corridor. If you lived on one side you could shake hands out the window with your neighbor on the other side across the stairs.

There was busy two-way traffic on the stairs. Women holding children or carrying things on their heads, children carrying groceries, a man wearing the orange overalls of a garbage collector, all scrambling up or going down. At the bottom of the stairs sat two boys. They fixed their eyes on Alex.

Were they spies? Alex wondered. He had heard that big drug bosses used boys and sometimes children as spies. They were supposed to warn people if there were police or strangers coming. The children did that because for a day's "work" they could get fries and steak or whatever they wanted. The boys said nothing.

Roy had said that he had to go all the way up. Out of breath, Alex climbed the last steps. He had climbed the entire flight of steps without a break and he was proud of himself. At the top the houses were made no longer of stone but of wood. Garbage lay all over the place and dishwater ran like a white ribbon over the path. But you had a beautiful view of the harbor. You could even see the bay and the sailboats.

"Yo, what're you doing here?"

Alex jerked his head around. On the path on the other side of the stairs stood a boy about his own age holding a pistol in his hand. Alex felt his legs shake. If only they didn't think he was a member of another drug gang.

"I'm looking for Walmir," he said in a tremulous voice. Walmir was the name Roy had given him.

The boy checked him out from head to toe. "What's your name?"

"Crusoe."

The boy didn't react. He motioned him up against the wall with his hands on his head. With his free hand he felt between Alex's legs, in his pockets, and under his T-shirt to see if he was carrying a weapon, and after that he turned him back around. "Wait here."

Another boy had come running up. This one carried a gun painted black over his shoulder. Was that an AR whatever, wondered Alex, the thing Big Mouth had been talking about? Then his eyes fell on his sneakers. He jumped. They were like the ones Big Mouth had had. No, they were Big Mouth's sneakers. His brain was running at top speed. How could this be?

Had Huff been the one, then? Huff and Roy were the only ones who regularly went up the hill to buy dope. But why had he taken Big Mouth's sneakers and given them to this boy? Had he made an exchange? For cocaine? Scissors had said something that had angered Huff. What was it again?

"Go get Walmir," said the first boy to the one with the sneakers. He stuck his pistol into the elastic waistband of his shorts.

Alex breathed with relief. Everything seemed to be in order and they knew Walmir. He wouldn't dream of asking about Huff and the sneakers. What if they started making trouble for him.

Walmir looked exactly the way Roy had described him. A little man wearing a purple T-shirt, with light-colored eyes and a scar on his cheek. He was carrying a knapsack, one of those brightly colored ones made of nylon that rich kids took when they went to school and that Alex had always wanted.

"How you doing. Everything all right, Crusoe?" He slapped Alex on the back as if he had known him for years. "Roy told me that you're a good friend of his. Reliable …" He paused and looked at Alex. "Knows his way around …"

Alex nodded. He didn't know what to say.

"Did Roy explain where you're supposed to bring this package?"

Alex nodded again. He was supposed to go to Flamengo Park. Another man would be waiting for him there.

"If all goes well, maybe you can work for us some more. Then you can make some money, buy clothes, and help out your mother. In a little while you can buy her a nice house. Where does your mother live?"

"I don't have a mother. She's dead," said Alex.

"I'm sorry to hear that. Who's taking care of your brothers and sisters?"

"I don't have any brothers and sisters."

"Oh." The man didn't seem to know what to say. "But I can see you're a fine boy. You won't let yourself be pushed around."

Slimeball, thought Alex. He shifted his weight impatiently from one leg to the other and looked at the bay. He didn't want to listen. Once you're in the business, you know for sure you're going to die young, his mother had said. He wanted to live.

"So, Crusoe, you're going to deliver this nice and clean. We're counting on you," said the man. "And you know what we do to rats," he added. His voice sounded ominous.

Alex nodded. He took the knapsack, nodded good-bye to the trio, and started his descent.

On the way back he took quiet streets. He tried to walk normally. Not too fast and not too slow, otherwise he would stand out. He also had to wear a normal expression. But what was his normal expression? He had never tried to see. Alex started humming.

> Just wanna feel fine
> Walkin' down the line,
> Down in the ghetto where I was born.

A street vendor standing behind a table covered with candy and cigarettes looked at him. Did the man know what was in his knapsack? Did Alex look like an *aviao*, a drug runner?

At every car he heard behind him his stomach did a flip. If he got caught by the police now, he was done for. Then he'd be a drug offender. They would send him to jail. They beat and kicked you there. They had gangs there. Anybody who didn't obey got their fingers chopped off, they said. Alex's legs were walking but his head was somewhere else. He thought of the horrible death awaiting him. It was better out on the street.

"Watch where you're going!"

He jumped. Because he was thinking about other things, he had bumped into a man. There was a loud cackling sound. A live chicken was trying to escape from the nylon shopping bag the man was carrying.

"Excuse me, sir," said Alex and he headed off. It made him think of the time he had been beaten by the police. That shouldn't happen again. He would start to count, then his mind wouldn't be able to think of anything else.

His heart leapt when he saw the man sitting in the park. It was just as Roy had said.

"What's your name?" Alex asked. Those were the orders Roy had given him.

"Alexander," said the man, as agreed. "You're Crusoe."

"Yes, I'm Crusoe." Alex took off the knapsack. On the way he hadn't dared to look, but from the feel of it, it weighed at least three kilos. That had to be worth a lot of money.

The man opened the knapsack, looked in, then stuck his hand in and felt around.

Alex waited.

"Fine," the man said. He slung the knapsack over his shoulder and groped in his pocket. "This is for you. Hey, thanks again."

Alex was holding three ten-*real* bills in his hand. He quickly looked around to see if anybody had seen him getting money. He saw only a man reading the paper under a tree. He folded up the bills very small and stuck them way down in his pocket. What if Dona Lica had happened to come by, or somebody else who knew him? As he was walking back, he decided he would never do it again. He'd tell Roy, You go up there yourself. He didn't want to have anything to do with drug people.

Rich

When you have money, the world changes in a heartbeat. Alex went and sat on the terrace of the first café he passed. The waiter rushed over to his table. By his frown you could tell that he wanted to chase Alex away.

"How much is the lasagna?" Alex asked quickly. Lasagna was his favorite food. His mother always made it with a lot of cream and cheese on top. He could eat nothing but lasagna for a whole month.

"Well, do you have money?" asked the waiter.

Alex pulled a crumpled ten-*real* bill out of his pocket.

"Hm," said the waiter and he walked away. A moment later he came back with a big dark brown folder. He laid it on the table and turned around without a word.

Alex opened the folder and was shocked. There were pages

typed full of gray words. MENU was written at the top. Running his finger along, he started reading from the top left. En-tree a la carte. Two fifty-six. What that was, he didn't know. He went on. Che-ese balls with butter. One fifty-three. Lunch spe-cial. Monday. Ground beef with ma-shed pot-a-toes. Tuesday. Beef stew with rice and roas-ted pot-a-toes.

He took a deep sigh. The gray mush hurt his eyes and made him sweat. He had never been very good at reading. When the waiter returned he had reached fish balls. Lasagna he hadn't seen yet. But he wasn't going to say that.

He slapped the menu shut. "A soda and a lasagna for me. I don't need a glass for the soda."

The waiter pulled the menu out of his hands and disappeared.

Noon had come and gone, and out on the terrace hung the smell of fried meat. The waiter placed platters on the table next to him. Alex looked at the door. When would his food come?

Time had never passed so slowly. He counted to a hundred, tried to ride a pebble on his big toe, laid out little houses with the toothpicks on the table, picked the dirt out from under his nails, thought about Duda, counted how many buses stopped at the square, counted how many passengers got on the bus, thought again about Duda, got rid of the toothpick houses and laid out trees with lots of branches, and then came the food.

"Perhaps you can clear away the toys?" said the waiter. "Then I can put your plate down." He pointed at the toothpicks.

Scumbag, thought Alex. But he did as he was told. The only thing that counted now was the lasagna: lots of it, warm and fragrant. He wanted to put the toothpicks back neatly into the little pot, but the waiter snatched it off the table.

"You don't really think people are going to want to put those things you had in your hands into their mouths, do you? It could make them sick!"

With a loud clatter he let the metal platter land on the table. "Here. Pay up, please. Nine *real*."

Alex ate it all. He could have kept on eating until his stomach burst. Hot food that fills you up. He couldn't remember the last time he had eaten a real meal. Maybe six months ago. In any case, before his mother had gone to the hospital.

He walked slowly in the direction of the square. In a display window he looked bigger, or was he imagining it?

The sidewalk was crowded with stalls. Between two trees a rope had been stretched and there were soccer jerseys hanging from it. They had all the teams and of course the Canaries' jersey, the yellow and green one of the Brazilian national team. "Twelve," said a woman who stuck her head out between the jerseys. She kept staring at him as if she were afraid that he was going to pull a shirt off a hanger and take off.

But Alex hadn't been thinking of that at all. Twelve *real*? He could easily afford that. How much he had wanted a soccer jersey during the World Cup! But his mother was already in the hospital and he had no money.

"Do you have number eleven?" If he was going to get one, then obviously he would get Romario's number.

The woman fanned through the shirts. "I got it. Let's see. Medium, yes, that'd be your size."

He hadn't yet decided, but when she held the Romario shirt out for him, he was sold. He felt rich when he pulled the two bills out of his pocket.

At a vendor's table on the next corner he bought a toy car for Bruno for two *real*. Why, he didn't exactly know. He was homesick. But how was he going to get it to Bruno?

Suddenly a thought flashed through his mind: if God wanted him to give the car to Bruno, he would surely let him live. Because who else was going to bring the car to Japeri? God will let me live because I have to bring the car. He said it aloud a couple of times as if he wanted to convince himself.

That night Alex did something he had never done before. He went to sleep in a hotel. He knew that there were cheap hotels behind the Central Station. It cost five *real* for a room to yourself. It was still light out when he went to sleep, but he didn't care. First he took a shower down the hall. He locked the door to his room and just to be sure he leaned a chair against it. Then he turned on the radio, because he even had one of those. He drew the curtains, laid the plastic bag with the Romario shirt and the little car for Bruno beside his pillow, and lay down in his clothes on the foam-rubber mattress. First on his back and then on his side, because that felt best after all. He tried to see how deep his finger would go into the mattress. Even when it went in really deep, it still hadn't reached the bottom. A thick mattress like that he had never had. He hoped his mother was awake. Hi, Mom, see me lying here? I even have a radio.

Alex was woken up the next morning by the sound of a running faucet. A faucet? he thought. Where am I? In Japeri there hadn't been any faucets. The window was different too. He looked around. Where was the door? When he saw the chair, he suddenly remembered everything.

He got up reluctantly. Now he had to go back to the street. Tonight he would once again be sleeping on stones with one eye open. Everything would start all over again. At the thought he despaired. If he were to carry another packet, he could … No, he wasn't going to think about that. He would do it three, five, ten times and then they would shoot and kill him. He saw the feet with the flip-flops again lying under the newspaper. Stealing was better, because there were really old thieves around.

He crossed the almost empty square. It was Sunday and

downtown was dead. There was a bakery that was open. There he had breakfast for eighty *centavos*, coffee with milk in it and a buttered roll. The plastic bag with the Romario shirt and the little car he placed in front of himself on the counter so that everybody could see that he wasn't a street kid. They don't go shopping.

As he was walking over to the square, he carefully sniffed his arm. He had even had soap at the hotel. Of course he had grabbed it. As he had the ashtray and the light bulb. Maybe he could sell them. It was too bad that the blanket had been so big, otherwise he would have taken that too.

In Santa Luzia Street everything was closed. An alcoholic lay on the ground sleeping. He lifted the manhole cover. He had to hide the Romario shirt and the little car very well or they would be ripped off. He laid everything down in the bottom under a newspaper. He hesitated with the car. But what if he should lose it? No, he was going to leave it in the hole.

He took out his bag with clothes. Now that he'd taken a real shower, he wanted to put on clean clothes. With the bag under his arm he headed over to the fountain.

Duda Again

He saw her from a distance even before he had reached the police box. Duda! She was back! She was bending over with her back to him near the edge of the fountain. Like a wild man he ran across the street, waving his plastic bag.

She was scrubbing Roy's elephant T-shirt and saw him only when he was standing beside her.

"Hey, Crusoe. How you doing?" Her whole face smiled.

Alex squeezed her arms with joy. "You were gone a long time." She was wearing a tight flowered T-shirt that was new. Her navel kept peeping out from under it. Her hair seemed different too. He never wanted to let her go away again.

"Ow, man, you're hurting me."

He was startled. Hurting Duda was the last thing he wanted to do. "How's your mother, Duda?"

"She's better," she said. "She's going to go away with my father," she added. "I'm going to help her make money when she moves. She's taking my sisters and my brother, they're still little."

Alex didn't know what to say. He felt a wet towel on his heart. If Duda went to help her mother, she was going back home. Then she would be gone.

He looked at her brown arms that shone with the water and hoped he hadn't heard right. She couldn't go away.

"When is your mother going?" Alex asked carefully.

"Ah, I don't know yet. She has to find a house first. That isn't easy."

Alex breathed in relief. Who knew, it might take a year and he might still live that long.

They scrubbed together for a time. She, Roy's T-shirts and shorts. He, his own clothes.

Then he took a chance. "I want to show you something."

She looked up at once. "What did you jack?"

"No. That isn't it. I want to show you a place. The most beautiful place in Rio."

Duda had gone back to scrubbing.

"You can go sunbathing there and fishing. And let your clothes dry and … there are monkeys and tigers and flying fish."

It worked. She stopped. "So where is it? The zoo, right? Tigers in the city. That's impossible, man."

"No, it isn't the zoo."

"I'm not going to the zoo. That's for children."

"It isn't the zoo. It's real close. We can walk."

She looked at him questioningly. "And what about the clothes?"

"They can dry out there."

Duda collected her washing and squinted around the square.

"Oh well, I don't see Roy anyway."

Alex was whooping inside. She was coming.

There they were, the two of them walking: she with a dripping plastic bag and he with wet clothes over his arm. He told her about Pear and Captain and of course about the devil doll. Every time she laughed a warm breeze blew through his head. In the park it was crowded. Sunday was family day. There were grandmothers with their grandchildren, fathers and mothers with children on little bicycles or held in their arms, and on the low walls boys whistling at girls. He didn't care; he was with Duda.

At the pier some people were roasting meat. Alex went ahead of Duda as they climbed on the rocks. "Here, Duda, this is a big rock. You can stand here."

Out on the point he selected a nice flat stone to sit on and he spread out his wet clothes.

"So now where are those tigers?" she asked.

He turned around and squinted down the stones. "Look, there."

She looked. "Ah, but that's a cat."

"It's a tiger."

"If that's a tiger, I'm a princess," she joked.

"But you are."

She jabbed him in the ribs. "You terrible liar. I knew it!"

They watched an airplane land. The hot air trembled under the landing gear. In the bay a speedboat whizzed by. The waves slapped and they quickly had to climb higher up so as not to get wet.

"Crusoe, why did you run away when your mother died?"

He started. She had never asked him anything like that before. The shouting on the beach was not more than a murmur out on the pier. On the footpath a police cruiser bored its way through the crowd.

"My stepfather didn't want me in the house. He had this thing against me." He fell silent.

"But how could he do that?" Duda sounded indignant. "You're so sweet and you're only thirteen. He couldn't just leave you to fend for yourself!"

Alex looked at her. It seemed as if she meant it. Then he told her everything. He told her that his mother wasn't his real mother but his foster mother. How the guy had come three years before and how he had bullied Alex away.

Alex told Duda about his mother, who had always worked herself to the bone as a cleaning woman to be able to buy rice and beans. When he got to the fights, he began to stutter. His head grew hot when he thought of the guy's lies. How the guy always blamed Alex for everything. How the guy had told his mother that he stole money, that he came home late at night, that he was a criminal. That she should throw him out of the house because he would cause her misery. She shouldn't believe Alex, the guy said.

Whenever his mother stayed overnight in the city, Alex didn't go home. Or else he would climb through the hole in the back wall on the sly so the guy wouldn't notice he was home.

When she went into the hospital, he came home even less. He washed his clothes in the river and ate mangos and bananas out in the country and leftovers from other people's plates.

"A little bit like now," said Duda. She had been quietly listening the whole time.

"No, no," he protested vehemently. "It was different. Now there's nothing to look forward to. My mother was alive then. We had lots of plans. When she got out of the hospital she was going to get a divorce. She was looking for a house. We'd go and live there, together with Bruno."

"Who's Bruno?"

Alex told her about Bruno and his other, older brother, Pito. "I'm sure the guy is bullying Bruno out of there right now. He wants the house for his own family."

"But why didn't you go live with Pito?" Duda wanted to know. "You fight with him?"

Alex shook his head. "His wife doesn't like me. Besides, they have a tiny house, two kids, and no money."

"I'll help you, though, Crusoe," said Duda. "I don't have any money either, but we're friends." She said it seriously. Without wanting to he thought of Robson. He was a friend too, but Alex hadn't seen him again.

"Duda, are street friends real friends?"

She thought for a long time.

"A lot of times they're not," she said finally. "They talk behind your back or they jack your things."

"Big Mouth's sneakers," said Alex. Would Duda know who had run off with them? he wondered.

"Exactly. But Big Mouth isn't so fine himself, you know. He ratted on me one time to the cops when he was caught. He pointed at me and said that I had yanked the purse. That wasn't true at all."

"And then?" asked Alex.

"They sent me to Santos Dumont. I was in there for three days, then I escaped."

"Escaped?" Alex immediately pictured little boats lying in the water waiting, disguised prison guards, and little saws baked into loaves of bread. "How?"

"Just climbed over the wall and then ran away fast."

Alex looked at her thin legs and imagined her lying on a wall three feet wide. He was proud of Duda.

"The street sucks," he said.

"But Santos Dumont is just a little bit worse," said Duda. "They beat you. It's dirty and the food is terrible. On the street at least you're free. You can do what you want."

"But there's nothing to do," said Alex. "You walk around and look at what other people are doing. Now what kind of a life is that? I'm bored to death most of the time!" he exploded.

"Should fall in love. Then you don't have enough time. You want to be kissing all the time," teased Duda.

"Like you, you mean."

"I'm married."

"Pah, married. Go tell that to the man in the moon. Where's the piece of paper, then?"

Duda acted as if she hadn't heard. "Roy wants to build a little house for us. Then we'll have children."

Alex looked at Duda's stomach and tried to imagine a baby growing inside. The stomach in the flowered T-shirt was much too small. It reassured him. That Roy could try what he wanted to, but a baby wouldn't ever fit.

They watched seagulls that let themselves float along on the waves and a fisherman in a rowboat hauling in his nets. He looked like a doll in a bottle cap compared to the oil tanker that was gliding by farther out.

"If you could choose between a plate of food and a bed, Duda, which would you choose?"

"You sure ask weird questions, Crusoe."

"Come on," he insisted.

"A bed."

"Me too," said Alex. "There's always some kind of food. Even if it's old bread or cold leftovers. But sleeping without having to be scared. Closing your eyes and forgetting, I like that a lot more. On the street you never get any rest." Alex thought of the little hotel room. Tonight somebody else would be lying in that bed. "The street is hell," he said.

"The street is good and the street is bad," said Duda. "You can go home as late as you want."

"I'd rather have a bed. If I had a bed, I'd go home every day at seven o'clock so that I could lie for a real long time in my bed."

"You're such a child," said Duda. "Life begins at night." She stretched out her legs. "The stones are nice and warm. I'm going to sleep for a little while. Are the clothes dry yet?"

"Jesus, where were you two?" Roy's eyes flashed fire when they came back to the fountain that evening. Alex had treated Duda to a hot dog with the last of his money, and they had split a can of soda.

"Crusoe let me see where he used to live," said Duda, "and then we stayed there to eat."

It was a white lie, thought Alex. But it sounded good.

Huff, Big Mouth, and Pear were lying on the ground sniffing glue. Scissors was lying on his side. He had rolled his blanket into a pillow.

"He's not doing too well," Roy said to Duda. He gave her a plastic bag with glue in it.

She sat down beside Scissors. Almost every time Scissors sniffed glue he got sick, and that had been going on for over a week.

"I want some too," said Scissors when he saw the plastic bag dangling above him.

"Boy, you're killing yourself. You got to lay off for a while, Scissors." Duda sounded stern. She kissed him on his forehead and stroked it.

"It's burning," said Scissors. "It's burning here." He pointed at his chest.

"He puked up everything today," said Pear.

Alex looked on from a distance. He was starting to get used to their sniffing glue every day. Once he had sniffed very quickly, but it had hurt a lot in his forehead. He had managed to stay away from it all the other times. Now the others didn't push him to sniff anymore and he kept to himself when they were sucking on their bags. If they said something, he didn't contradict them. If they nudged him, he didn't slap them away, because he was still scared of what could happen when they had sniffed themselves silly.

Alex was happy that Duda was back. Everybody seemed more cheerful.

When there were dirty clothes to be washed, Duda and Alex went to the fountain together to wash them. After that they would walk to the pier with the clothes, because Roy was often gone in the afternoon. There they would lie in the sun. It had come to be their spot.

They talked about the street, about past friends, about their mothers, or about nothing. Sometimes they made up stories about tigers, talking buildings, and time machines. But about Crusoe on the island, Alex had never told her. He knew better. What if she laughed at him? You're such a child. He could hear her saying it. He had never told Duda about the packet of cocaine either. He was ashamed of that.

"What do you do when you're sad, Duda?" Alex really wanted to know. Sometimes he wished he didn't have any feeling. That he was empty inside and would never have to think about Japeri again.

"When I'm sad, I close my eyes and imagine that I'm a bird."

"A bird?" Alex asked in surprise.

"Yeah, then you can fly anywhere and it doesn't cost a thing."

"Do you dream about later on too?"

"Then I'm a secretary," said Duda. "I'm wearing nylons and a tight skirt and I smile at everybody. I work in a big hotel and every day I get postcards. Because I've got friends in every country. At night I go home on the subway. My husband picks me up. He works in an office. He's big and strong and makes lots of money. We have a house with a bathroom in it."

"Is that man Roy?"

Duda looked at Alex. "Of course it's Roy. Who else?"

"And when you're hungry, what do you do then?" Alex quickly changed the subject. He didn't like Duda looking at him that way. Besides, he was hungry. His stomach was like a grunting pig.

"If I don't have any money?"

"Duh, of course. If you don't have any money."

"If I don't have any money, I ask somebody to buy something for me."

"But nobody wants to buy you anything and you're really, really hungry," Alex persisted. She was getting him all worked up.

"Then I go to the soup bus," replied Duda.

"But it isn't evening yet by a long shot," said Alex.

"Then I drink water," replied Duda.

Alex sighed. "But that doesn't help."

"Then I go to the big airport."

The big airport was far outside the city. Alex, lying on the rocks, turned his face toward Duda. She always had exciting answers. What would be next? Duda looked at the sky and pretended she hadn't noticed anything.

"Why do you go to the big airport? C'mon, tell me!"

Duda giggled. "A tip from Huff," she said.

She told him about Huff hearing that you could eat really well at the big airport. Behind one of the airport buildings there was a long white wall. Behind it stood garbage cans. In the cans was all the food that people hadn't eaten on the airplanes. Together with the others Duda had climbed over the wall.

"So much food, Crusoe. Chicken with sauce, meat, pudding. Real soft sweet rolls, spaghetti, shrimp. They got everything there. All in those little boxes or bags. Opening them up is a lot of work. But Jesus, Crusoe, how we ate over there." Duda looked up dreamily.

"Yeah," said Alex. "But for the big airport you have to take two buses." What good was a solution like that to him? He was hungry now. "I'm hungry," he said. "Let's go ask for some food."

Duda looked at him. "I don't ask, I take."

Alex knew she was telling the truth. Duda shoplifted everything. She even lifted on order. She'd put on a skirt and go into the Mesbla. When the salespeople weren't looking, she would tuck the prize between her legs. T-shirts, cassette tapes, shampoo. After that she would walk out of the store very carefully. For Roy she had ripped off a Walkman. Big Mouth's baseball cap had also been snagged by Duda. But that she had snatched off a street vendor's table.

The clothes were dry. With their plastic bags under their arms they walked back.

"Watch," said Duda when they were on Gloria Street. She walked a few steps ahead of him. She let her right arm dangle loosely at her side. When she reached a stall with oranges, her arm shot out like a tentacle. And off went Duda with two oranges.

On the Attack

Stealing was getting easier and easier for Alex. Going up to cars at the traffic lights he thought was scary. He was afraid that somebody would shoot him. At night he went up the street with a broken bottleneck. Then they couldn't see his face so well. If you were black you had an advantage in the dark, said Big Mouth. He was right, Alex thought. He struck in alleys downtown, usually by himself. Sometimes with Huff, Big Mouth, or Pear along.

There were always people who worked late at the office. Usually he shoved the bottleneck under their chins. "Hand it over or I'll slice you to shreds," he would say.

He had also had some success with fireworks. He had poked one into the back of an old guy with a briefcase who was standing at a store window. "If you turn around, I'll shoot," he had said. "Set the briefcase down on the ground." The guy had started trembling like a blade of grass and had immediately done what he had said. Alex had run away with the case and the man hadn't even yelled. If you're that stupid, you're asking to be robbed, Alex felt.

He was disgusted when he unzipped the case. There was nothing but papers in it. Nobody walked around with money, it seemed. In a side pocket he found a subway pass, two pens, and a vial of pills. One of the pens he gave to Duda, the other to Scissors. He kept the pills for himself. If he were to get sick, at least he had some medicine.

Alex had completely forgotten the pills until one evening when they were sitting by the fountain.

"We got to bring Scissors to the hospital," said Duda.

"I don't want to go to the hospital," yelled Scissors.

"So do you want to die?" said Duda. "You don't eat anything and you wander around all day puking."

"So I die."

Alex looked at Scissors' face. It looked even thinner than usual. Suddenly he remembered the pills. He ran to Santa Luzia Street.

"Where you going?" shouted Pear. But Alex didn't hear.

He had put them in the manhole. In the bag with the little car for Bruno. With a stick he flipped the cover open. Then he lay down on his knees and reached down with his arm to hook the bag up. It was lying all the way at the bottom.

He was shaking when he handed the vial over to Duda.

"Hey, Crusoe. Where'd you get these?" She looked happily surprised.

"Still had them."

"But maybe those pills are for something totally different," said Pear.

Duda walked over to the light pole and turned the vial around in the light.

"No, it won't work," she said when she came back. "It says 'Keep out of the reach of children' on it." She handed the vial back to Alex.

"But I'm not a child," said Scissors.

"So, what are you, man?" Big Mouth snorted. "A grown-up?"

"I'm a lion," Scissors said weakly.

They didn't have a chance to talk more because Huff came walking up over the grass. "Hey, is there still some huff?"

Huff slapped Alex and Big Mouth on the back and pinched Pear's cheek. "That's my honey." Duda, he blew a kiss. He should try that when Roy's around, thought Alex. What was up with Huff? Why was he in such a good mood? He looked at Huff's slightly stooped back as he and Big Mouth walked to the edge of the grass.

Alex liked Huff. Maybe it was because he had been abandoned by his mother. To Alex, that was the worst that could happen to you. Actually it was even worse than if your mother died, it occurred to him.

Huff hopped buses. That created a bond too. Alex had hopped trains when he was still living at home. OK, so it wasn't exactly the same thing. To hop trains you stood on the roof of the moving train, and to hop buses you had to hang. But it was almost as dangerous. You grabbed onto the handle beside the door, and when the bus picked up speed, you let yourself swing so your head almost touched the asphalt. But at the turns you had to come up quick or else your head would be smashed.

Huff, angry at the whole world, wasn't scared of anything. Whenever he walked past the police box on the square, he would spit on the ground. He faced Roy if something wasn't to his liking or if he thought he wasn't getting his share of glue or food.

Huff always walked around with a piece of glass in his pocket. One time they were interviewed by a newspaper journalist. Huff demanded three hundred dollars.

"Do you have any idea how much that is, three hundred dollars?" the young man said, chuckling. "I don't even make that much in a month."

As a reward for "services rendered," the journalist bought each of them a hamburger. Roy, who of course played the boss, also got five *real* to buy some soda. Which became glue.

Everybody was happy except Huff. "So how about it, man?" he kept on. "I'll send the Association of Street Children after you if you don't pay. They have a lawyer."

When the journalist got into his car, Huff had already stuffed his pockets with stones. And sure enough: pitterpat, clinkety clank. Three windows got it.

"Should have paid, greedy bloodsucker!" Huff shouted before he broke into a run.

Huff had balls, thought Alex. You could see that he'd been hardened by life.

What had Huff come up with this time? Everybody was standing around him.

"Look, Crusoe," said Huff when he had joined the others. He was holding something in his hand. He made a quick motion and suddenly he was holding a knife in his fist.

"It's fly, huh?" Huff lovingly ran his fingers along the steel and snapped the knife shut again.

"Where'd you get that?" asked Alex.

"Bought it on the street. Eight *real*."

"You'll get that money back in no time," said Big Mouth. "You pop a couple of old biddies in Copacabana. Let me see, Huff." He stuck out his hand. Carefully Huff laid the shut knife on the palm of his hand. He was acting as if it were a newborn baby, thought Alex. Huff was up to doing a lot of things, but was he able to stab somebody to death?

The knife kept the Angels occupied. Everybody wanted to lie down beside Huff when they spread out the cardboard in Santa Luzia Street for the night.

"Now you can really slam, Huff," said Pear. "Maybe even two hundred *real* a day."

"Two hundred *real?*" repeated Scissors, who had cheered up considerably. "Then you can buy a bicycle. Are you going to buy a bicycle, Huff?"

Huff, who was lying next to him, turned his head to the side. "Buy what? Some huff, you mean. If I make a lot of money, I'm going to have a party."

"I'd buy a house for my mother," Scissors fantasized.

Alex, who was lying on the outside, raised himself up. Scissors never talked about his mother.

Scissors was lying on his back. His eyes were gleaming strangely. He was talking more to himself than to Huff, it seemed. "Our house would have a TV and a tiled floor. I'd buy clothes for her, too, and a watch. And she could have anything she wanted to eat. Black beans with orange, meat, ice cream. She'd never have to work again. In the morning we'd watch television together."

Duda and Roy were having sex. Pear, who was lying beside Scissors, ran his hand over his forehead. But Scissors didn't seem to notice. He was staring up.

Alex lay back down. Was Scissors really sick? He hoped not. Suddenly he thought of the time Bruno had had pneumonia. How would he be now? He was most likely lying in his bed. Right after thinking about Bruno, Alex fell asleep.

A couple of days later Huff came running up the square all out of breath to where the others were sitting. It was the evening rush hour. On the wide street along the square, honking cars stood six deep. It was starting to get dark.

"The Platform Panthers, the Platform Panthers," he gasped.

"Yuck, the Platform Panthers." Pear made a nasty face.

"What's happening with the Platform Panthers?" asked Big Mouth.

"They huffed themselves into orbit this afternoon. Then they all forced their way into the church on the corner over there and smashed the benches to bits, then they ran across President Vargas Street and broke a bunch of windows over there, and then they formed an *arrastão*, an ambush."

Alex was alarmed. The thing he had been dreading for so long had happened. Except it hadn't been the Asphalt Angels.

"Fly!" said Big Mouth. "An *arrastão* on President Vargas Street. That must have been bad! People screaming. People on top of kiosks. Cars in line honking, passersby on the hoods." Big Mouth let his imagination have free rein.

"What else happened, Huff? How did it end up?" asked Duda.

"The cops came, of course. They hauled them off to the hospital. But they couldn't keep them shut up in there. They swore they'd trash the place again. And then they were let back out on the street."

"Fly," Big Mouth said again. "In the hospital. Vrooooom. Clinkety clank. What was that? A flying stretcher, nurse. Vrooooom. Clinkety clank. And what was that? A flying doctor, nurse."

Nobody laughed. The news had made a big impression.

"Jesus, Huff, what now?" asked Duda.

"What now? They're back home again. On the square. And on the corner of President Vargas Street there's a police wagon. You know, one of those police vans with grilles on the windows."

"Wow, they sure got balls, though," said Duda.

"Did they jack anything?" Pear wanted to know. He had been quietly listening the whole time.

"I don't know. The newspaper man on the station square says they did. They mugged about ten people."

Alex said nothing. The street gets everybody, he thought.

The Interview

The day after the outburst downtown a television crew showed up. When Alex got back from the beach, a big, shiny TV news van was parked in Santa Luzia Street. Men were walking up and down the arcade with lights and cords. Roy was busy talking with a fancy-looking lady. She looked like a movie star, thought Alex. She was holding a notepad in her hand and was writing down everything Roy said. She was nodding a lot.

Duda, Big Mouth, and Pear were sitting on the stoop watching.

"I'm going to be on television," Scissors crowed when he saw him. He hung on to Alex's arm. Scissors was almost entirely his old self.

"What do they want?" Alex asked.

"How should I know? We're going to be on television. Yay."

When Roy saw him, he motioned him over. "Crusoe, this girl wants to ask us a couple of questions in a little while."

Alex nodded. "Where's Huff?"

"He's getting some grip together."

The woman quickly wrote something down. "All right, I believe we can begin," she said, looking at the men with the cords.

"Can those children go over and sit on that piece of cardboard?" She pointed with her pen toward Duda, Big Mouth, Pear, and Alex.

"What does she mean, children?" said Big Mouth.

"Man, just do as you're told. OK?" said Roy.

Alex dropped down beside the others on the stoop.

"Yes, that's it. Close together. Where's that little one? A little one like that's cute."

Roy looked around. Scissors was skipping around the sidewalk in his T-shirt that was five sizes too big. To all the passersby he said, "I'm going to be on television."

When everybody was finally sitting down, the lights switched on.

Alex blinked in the bright light and felt a knot in his stomach. He hoped she wouldn't ask him anything. Was he supposed to say something about his stepfather? Maybe the guy was watching. Everybody was watching, of course. That hadn't occurred to him before. All of Japeri would see that he was a street kid! It was too late now. He was trapped in the light. The camera was rolling.

He saw that Roy was making a reply. The woman drew the microphone toward herself again.

"So you sniff glue too. But why do you do that when you know it's bad?"

She looked around. Duda raised her hand.

"When you huff glue, you don't feel anything. It's as if your body isn't yours anymore. You aren't hungry anymore; you don't think about the past anymore. It's a little like dreaming with your eyes open. It's a dream with lots and lots of color and everything's moving," said Duda.

"It's good for jacking, too. You're not scared at all anymore," Big Mouth added.

"But why did those other kids start smashing things up yesterday?" the woman insisted.

Scissors was bobbing back and forth. "I know this kid and he ate a blue plastic egg carton up when he was high on glue. Not the whole thing, but almost the whole thing."

"You mean one of those Styrofoam cartons?" The woman was looking at him in disbelief.

Scissors nodded vehemently.

"When you huff glue, you're not yourself anymore. You don't know what you're doing," explained Roy.

The woman fell silent. She looked alarmed.

"All right," she said. She cleared her throat. "Now let's talk about something else." She looked at Pear. "Can you put that blanket around you?"

Pear groaned. "It's much too hot. Does that bitch want me to suffocate?"

Roy, who was sitting behind him, jabbed him. The woman had Duda throw her arm around Scissors. Wildly Scissors tore himself away. "I'm not a baby. I'm ten."

"Well, well," said the woman. "You're ten. Do you steal too?"

Scissors gave her a withering look. "I don't steal. I borrow and then I don't give it back."

"And why do you steal?"

"I don't steal." Scissors was angry.

"I wasn't asking you," said the woman. She was pointing the

microphone at Pear.

Alex saw Pear swallow.

"Uhh," Pear began. "If you don't steal, how are you supposed to eat? Besides, rich people steal too. The water is everybody's, isn't it? If you have water in your house, you have to pay for it."

The woman pulled the microphone back. If only I don't have to go, thought Alex. He was sitting next to Pear.

"Why don't you polish shoes or sell candy? There are lots of children who work. You don't need to steal, do you?"

"Man, she nuts or what?" Big Mouth whispered to Alex. The woman looked around the group to see if anybody wanted to say anything. But it remained quiet.

"You over there. I heard you saying something?" She pointed at Big Mouth.

"Stupid bitch," Big Mouth cursed softly.

"Yes … ?" she said questioningly.

Big Mouth took a deep breath. "I'm not crazy. You don't make anything when you work. You're working and you still can't buy anything. If you polish shoes you get thirty *centavos*. On a good day you can do ten pairs. That's … three *real*. What's three *real*? So you got nothing, because the bus to and from home costs one-eighty. I'm not going to do that. I'm not retarded." He paused and looked around the group. They were quiet. "If you want to buy something, a T-shirt or kicks, you got to steal."

The woman checked her notepad and then her watch. "All right, two more questions."

Alex breathed easier. With a little bit of luck nobody would see him.

"There are people who want to take you off the street. There are also people who want to kill you because you're criminals. What's your opinion about this?"

Again it was quiet. Duda looked at her lap. Scissors had his thumb in his mouth. Alex, who had ducked back as far as possible, saw the camera slip from head to head. Roy stood up. Oh no, thought Alex. Now it's going to be official.

"We are not criminals. Criminals are the rich who steal and the police who kill. We steal to live. And the street belongs to everybody. We aren't leaving, because this is our home. We have just as much right as everybody else. Nobody has to worry about us because we take care of ourselves. We help one another. We, the Asphalt Angels, are like one big family. Angels don't die. Because when we die, there'll be new Asphalt Angels."

Scissors clapped loudly. "Roy, Roy, Roy!" he cheered. Roy smiled shyly and sat down. Duda was looking at him with admiration. That Roy sure could talk, thought Alex. He could be a politician any day.

The woman exchanged a glance with a man wearing headphones.

"Can we have some quiet here for a moment?" she said while she looked sternly at Scissors. "The final question: what do you want to be?"

"Police officer," shouted Scissors. "Because then you can steal and nobody can catch you." The others had to laugh.

The woman held the microphone up to Big Mouth.

"I'm not going to be anything," said Big Mouth. "I'm going to die young anyway."

"I didn't ask you what you thought you would be but what you want to be," she said.

"What do I want to be?" Big Mouth looked surprised. It seemed as if he had never thought about that before. "I'd like to be … a musician. A rap musician."

"And you? We haven't heard from you at all."

Alex's heart skipped two beats. The microphone stopped in front of his chest. He had to say something. But what had she asked? He felt burning hot. She stared at him and her eyes were saying, Say whatever is on your mind.

"I, uh." He took a deep breath. "I want a bed and a mother. That's what I want most of all." She nodded at him in a friendly way and took the microphone away.

Thank God, thought Alex. It's over.

"No, no," screamed the woman when they wanted to get up. "Now some separate shots. Go over there and lie in front of that bar. Where are the glue bags, Oscar?" The man with the cords placed a cardboard box with bags of glue in it on the sidewalk.

"And now you all pretend you're sniffing glue. Yes, that's right. Close your eyes as if it were real … Enough? All right, kids. We've got enough. Thank you."

The spotlight went out and the shiny TV news van drove away. Within fifteen minutes everything was the way it always was.

Well, not completely. The Angels were exuberant. They sat by the fountain and talked about nothing else. Huff's coming back with a can of glue and cocaine didn't seem to interest anybody. They shouted over one another to tell him everything. "Can we have some quiet here for a moment?" With his high voice Pear imitated the woman.

"I want a mother. I want a mother," cried Big Mouth. The others rolled around in the grass they were laughing so hard.

"You were the bomb, man," Duda said to Roy.

Big Mouth gave Roy a slap on the back. "You told those guys who abuse kids the truth. I hope they're watching. Angels don't die!"

When evening came they moved to a café Roy knew well in a dark little street behind the square. There was a television there. The woman had said that it would be broadcast that same evening.

"Action against street children in Rio," the news anchorman with the white hair announced. Alex recognized him immediately because in Japeri he had watched a lot of television.

"That's us!" yelled Scissors, who was sitting on the floor.

"Quiet," snapped Roy.

There were images of smashed-up benches in the church, people running, and street kids in the ambulance. Then the woman came on screen. "After the *arrastão*...downtown Rio... juvenile court judge ... take children off the streets ... youth homes spread out over the city..."

A man who was sitting at a desk came on screen. "I know him," cried Duda. "That's the juvenile court judge. He's the one who sent me to Santos Dumont."

The judge was talking. He talked about the interests of the children. Responsibility of society.

Then the woman came on again. She was standing in Santa Luzia Street. "Downtown ... more than a hundred street children ... plague the neighborhood ... robberies ... fear." She asked a man a question.

"Fatso?" said Big Mouth in surprise. Fatso, round as a beachball, was the owner of a restaurant on the corner of Santa Luzia Street.

"Ssshhh," the others hissed in unison.

"... criminals ... customers stay away... their rights ... we also have rights ..."

"What'd he say now?"

"Duda, that's you lying there." Scissors jumped up.

Duda with a glue bag in a zoomshot and after that Pear and then Scissors. "Me. Yay. I'm on television."

"Sshh."

Again the woman came on. "... lying on the street in the

shopping district … addicted … steal … getting some grip together."

Alex pricked up his ears. Had he understood right? Had she said that one of them went out stealing while the others sniffed? "'Getting some grip together,' the way they say it themselves." So that was what she had written down when he had asked about Huff.

Duda came into view again. This time she was talking: "You're done for on the street anyway," she said. After that it was Big Mouth's turn. "It's good for jacking, too. You're not scared at all anymore." Then Pear came on. "If you don't steal, how are you supposed to eat?"

Alex was relieved. He hadn't been on. Now you could see the street again. The Angels were sitting on the stoop. Alex saw only a tiny bit of his hair and his cheek. The woman stepped in front of the camera. "These children are looking forward to moving." She said it loud and clear. After that Alex came into view.

"I want a bed and a mother. That's what I want most of all."

It was quiet for a second. Then all hell broke loose.

"Liars. Sleazy journalists. They twist everything." Roy was shouting and he slammed his fist on the table. Alex had never seen Roy so angry.

Duda patted him on the back. "Easy there."

Pear got up. "Are they going to take us off the street? That's what that woman said, isn't it?"

Roy nodded. "The juvenile court judge said he was going to send vans through the city to pick up all the kids. He's going to lock us up. 'Youth homes,' he calls it. But it's the same thing as being institutionalized."

"Jesus. Not me. Then I'll go back to my mother." Big Mouth was shocked.

"And you know what those liars on television say: that we're looking forward to it. That that's what we really want," said Roy.

Scissors was still sitting on the floor; he was crying quietly. "I...don't...want to be institutionalized."

"What are we going to do now, Roy?" Pear sounded desperate. "It's all because of Exu. We shouldn't ever have touched that doll. I knew it."

Alex said nothing. It was his fault. He had said, I want a mother.

Trapped

They were lying on their pieces of cardboard in the arcade. Alex looked at the pavement. A silvery VW bug drove by. Aside from that, the street was empty. Empty, it suddenly looked twice as wide. Alex couldn't help thinking about what Roy had said. Alex had no family, so he would be institutionalized for sure. And who was going to get him out again? Big Mouth could ask his mother. Huff had his grandmother. But he had nobody. Alex felt like the loneliest person in the world.

In any case he would lie if they asked if he had stolen. Maybe that would help. Who knows, maybe they had two places. One for thieves where they chopped off your fingers and another where you could play soccer and get food three times a day.

Tomorrow he would burn a candle for his mother and then he would ask her if he could go to the place where you could play soccer. If there was such a thing, of course. But he shouldn't forget to say that he'd rather not go to any place at all.

He looked beside him. He wasn't the only one who had problems. Only Scissors was asleep. All the others had their eyes open.

"Everybody's against us," said Roy. "The police, the judge, Fatso, the reporters, the Platform Panthers, those guys who abuse kids and throw gasoline around."

"Why is Fatso against us?" asked Huff.

"Didn't you see it on TV? He said we stole stuff and chased his customers away," said Roy.

"How can he say that? If there's any jacking going on in this street, it's got to be somebody else. We don't do nothing. We stick to our deals."

"You know what I think?" said Duda with a frown. "Somebody's doing it on purpose. Because he's against us. He wants us run out."

"The Platform Panthers," said Huff. "Underhanded bunch."

"Maybe he's doing it himself. I mean, hiring somebody."

"Oh, Duda," said Roy. "Fatso never said a word. Why would he want to get rid of us? If you ask me, you're imagining things."

Duda snorted and rolled over. She sure is angry, thought Alex.

A car was driving up. Everybody suddenly stopped talking. It drove on.

"See that?" said Huff.

"What?" asked Roy.

"That bug. It's the second time that car's gone by. You can't see who's inside because it has tinted windows. You think they're up to something?"

"From now on we have to pay better attention at night," said Roy.

Alex was thinking the same thing. "Let's stand guard in turns," he suggested. "But for real."

"We have to get out of here," said Big Mouth. He had said hardly a word the entire evening. "They'll probably be sending those vans downtown first. Let's go to Copacabana."

Huff protested. "Naw, man. You, maybe, but not me. Those Germans there won't ever let you in. That's war, as soon as you cross into their turf."

"Yeah, that's true," said Big Mouth. "But where else can we go?"

It was quiet for a minute. Alex looked at Duda. Her back wasn't moving. Maybe she was asleep.

"I think I have an idea," said Roy. "But I'm not going to say anything yet. I have to check it out first."

What was it, Alex wondered. Roy had lots of contacts. Maybe they would all go live in a house together. Roy had said that the Angels were one big family, hadn't he?

Alex woke up at five-thirty. The doorman was tossing buckets of soapy water out over the pavement. The shutters of the bar were rolled halfway up. Everything seemed the same, but it wasn't. With a jolt he recalled the previous evening. They were coming to get them. Sleeping was impossible; there was doom in the air.

At a bar in the street behind the square he asked for water and coffee. In a trash can he found a buttered roll in a paper bag. He ate it on a stone bench in the square. A police van was parked at the movie theater. What was going to happen? Was there a demonstration going on today? In the square two officers were walking around with a dog. That was weird too. He had never seen officers with a dog in the square before.

"Hey, man," said Huff, sitting down next to Alex. Huff's eyes were bloodshot. "You see that?" He nodded in the direction of the police van.

"Yeah."

"Damn, man, this stinks. We've had it."

"But how do you know that van's for us?" asked Alex.

"Don't you see it, man? First Fatso says we bag on people, then that bug with the black glass, and now cops in the square and a cop van. There's never any cop vans parked by the square." Huff sniffed deeply.

Alex was silent. Huff always had the feeling that the police were after him. But Alex was getting a little nervous himself. Could they stick him into a police van if he just sat here and did nothing wrong? Could they pick him up because he didn't have an ID? But there were lots of kids who didn't have papers. Alex didn't know the answer.

Huff had walked away and come back again. "There's two goons sitting in that van."

"You see? Two, that's not enough by far for seven street kids."

"And that dog. You see that dog? This stinks, man. I'm telling you, this stinks." He tapped his foot restlessly on the tiles. "If it goes on like this, I'm history. They won't get me. The people from the business want me to work with them. Then I'll be making money. I'll have a nice life before I die, anyway. Always some huff, women, clothes, money. Better than this shit here."

Alex looked at him searchingly. "But weren't you supposed to be able to go back where you lived?"

"No. I'm going somewhere else. It's the people at the Morro da Providencia that asked me. Where you were too one time."

Alex said nothing. He didn't want to be reminded of the trip with the knapsack. How did Huff know about that anyway? Had Roy told him?

In the square, waiters set chairs out on the terraces. At lunchtime they would all be filled.

The police van was still there.

"So aren't you scared of dying?" asked Alex.

"Shit, man, sure. But you think I want to be in one of those places? I'm not going to let myself get butchered on the street. I'm going to fight back."

It was quiet for a moment. Then Huff said in a low voice, "I'll get a twelve millimeter if I work with them."

"A twelve millimeter? What's that?"

"A gun, man. Sure can tell you're from the sticks! It's double-barreled. So when you shoot, two bullets come out. When they come at me, I'll blast them dead."

"Hey there, what're you two whispering about?" Duda stuck her head in between them. She was with Pear.

"Where are you two going?" asked Alex.

"Hey, you are curious, aren't you," said Duda. Pear giggled.

"Women," said Huff and he heaved a sigh.

Duda looked at him, offended, and then said to Alex, "We're going to see a friend of Pear's. He sells flip-flops on the street in Lapa. After that we're going to São Martins. They got free food there at noon."

"São Martinho," Pear corrected her.

"Oh yeah. São Martinho."

"What's that?"

"Pear heard that they have hot food there every day at twelve for street kids. There's a cantina and you can just go in."

"But they ask your name and you have to talk with a sss—" Pear stamped his foot. "What's that called again, a ssss—"

"A social services representative?" asked Duda.

"Yeah, a social services representative." Pear was visibly relieved.

"And that's what you're going to go do?" Huff shook his head. "You're being totally stupid. What do you think they're going to do with your name? They hand it over to the cops. Or they go to your parents. You won't see me in there. You come back the next day, the goons are waiting for you. I'm not dumb."

"That's not true!" Pear was angry. "I know a guy and he goes there every day. And he boosts too."

"Forget about him, he's full of it," said Duda. "Coming, Crusoe?"

Alex shook his head. He didn't know what he wanted. He felt funny.

He spent the day on the beach and on the pier. He hauled beer, for which he got paid two *real*. After that he went to lie on the rocks and thought about what he should do. He didn't know. What could he do?

Huff was right. On the street you were done for. If you were in the business, at least you had a nice life until you were shot dead. But Huff had balls and he didn't. He'd pee in his pants if he had a weapon in his hands. He was scared of people in the business, scared of the police and scared of getting hooked. But he was particularly scared of the future. If there was one. Maybe he'd be dead tomorrow.

At the Gloria Church he bought a candle from a big black woman for twenty *centavos*. He stuck it on the sidewalk and burned it for his mother. It was the first time he had lit a candle for her. He felt a lot lighter when he walked to the square.

The Angels were not around the fountain as they usually were. He walked around on the square. They weren't there either. They wouldn't have been picked up by that van? His heart was pounding. It couldn't be true. Then he saw them. Pear, Huff, and Big Mouth were sitting on the steps of the museum. Scissors was tightrope-walking on the chainlink fence around the green. What was going on, wondered Alex. They didn't have any glue and they seemed so quiet. And where were Duda and Roy?

"Duda got picked up," said Pear without looking up when Alex flopped down beside them on the steps.

"Picked up?"

"Yeah, taken away by the police."

"How's that?" Alex couldn't believe it. Beautiful Duda. Duda with the strong brown arms. His Duda.

Pear told him how he had gone into the Mesbla with Duda. Pear had distracted the salesperson in the music department and then Duda had quickly tucked a Walkman between her legs. Duda was the first to walk out. Halfway to the exit a man had grabbed Duda by the shoulder. The Walkman had fallen on the floor. Another man had come over with a dark uniform on. The two of them had taken Duda away. Pear had waited on a wall in front of the Mesbla. After a time a squad car had come. A policeman had gone to get Duda from inside. They had put her in the car and she was gone. She hadn't seen Pear.

It was as if Alex's head had started to float, it became so light. That stupid Duda. Why had she let herself get caught? How could she have left him all alone?

"And now?"

"Nothing," said Pear and he dejectedly shrugged his shoulders. "Roy's gone to find out where she is. He knows a straight cop." Big Mouth, who was sitting below him, was shooting pebbles across the sidewalk.

"If you get caught shoplifting they send you to Padre Severino," said Huff flatly. "But Duda's a girl, so she gets to go to Santos Dumont."

"But Duda'll escape. She's smart," said Alex. "She escaped once before."

Huff looked at him in disbelief.

"Batman's going to save Duda," said Scissors, who had come over to sit with them. "He'll jump on the roof. His cape'll be flapping around because there's a strong wind on the roof. And then they come out to get some exercise. Then he beams this message to Duda. And then she looks up and wwhhhtt, there comes this rope. She grabs hold of it and vvrroooom, she's gone. Batman waves and vvrroooom, and then he's gone too."

"Cut it out, Scissors, cut the crap. It's no time for jokes," said Huff. "There's no such thing as Batman."

Scissors pouted. "Is so."

Alex was silent. He knew nothing about prisons. He hoped they wouldn't hurt Duda.

Santos Dumont

The days following Duda's pick-up, Alex went off by himself more often. As he used to, he sat on the pier for hours watching the boats and the flying fish. He was angry and sad at the same time. It wasn't fair. Why did all the good people disappear from his life? His mother, Robson, and now Duda. In the gang everything was a little bit different. Roy had talked everybody's spirits up the first night. "We're sticking together. They won't break us up. We're a family and I'll make sure Duda comes back." During the day Roy was gone a lot, and at night he took his time getting back. It was usually Huff who arranged for the glue. Big Mouth and Huff argued a lot.

Pear also missed Duda badly. Alex could tell from everything he did. He often sat quietly on the square and had a lot less to say. The only one you couldn't tell anything from was Scissors.

But he was a child. Scissors was as cheerful as before and spent most mornings by the television store.

In the square everything looked normal again. The officers with the dog and the police van had disappeared. There was no more talk about the vans that were going to come and institutionalize them. Had the Angels forgotten? wondered Alex. He hadn't forgotten. Every day he wanted to ask Roy how things stood, where they were going to go, but he kept forgetting. But Roy always got back so late.

It was over a week since Duda had been arrested and it was getting toward one o'clock. Alex and Pear were sitting in the square eating chicken and rice. That morning they had robbed a woman standing in front of a movie theater looking at the posters.

"Crusoe, Crusoe."

Alex glanced up from his container and saw only waving arms at first but then the bush of orange curls. It was Scissors. He was zigzagging in his bare feet between people. His T-shirt flapped around his skinny body.

Panting, he stood next to the bench. He flapped both arms in his excitement. "Duda ... Duda."

Alex stopped eating at once. "Duda? Let's have it, Scissors. What's with Duda?"

"I sawhaw Duda ahand ..." panted Scissors. And then he had a coughing fit.

Pear slapped him on the back. "Easy, Scissors. Take deep breaths."

It took several minutes before Scissors caught his breath. For Alex it seemed like hours. Then Scissors told them that he had seen Duda on television. She was in a courtyard, she was wearing a uniform, and she spoke.

"But you know for sure it was Duda?" asked Alex.

Scissors nodded.

"And what did she say?"

"How would I know? The TV's in the store, dummy. Outside on the street you can't hear anything." Scissors looked sideways at him, surprised at so much stupidity.

"What'd she look like?"

Scissors thought for a minute. "Like Duda. Yeah, she looked like Duda. You know, pretty."

Alex sighed. You couldn't count on Scissors for this kind of thing.

Pear mumbled. "I'll bet she's in Santos Dumont."

Alex was happy that there were signs of life from Duda. But Roy looked devastated when the boys told him the news. They were sitting at their usual spot on Santa Luzia Street. Scissors had repeated what he had seen.

"We have to get her out," said Big Mouth right away.

"Sure, but first we have to know where she is exactly," said Roy. He thought for a moment. You could tell by his forehead that a plan was brewing. His eyebrows wiggled up and down. "I'm going over there. I'll say I'm Duda's brother and that we saw her on television. She ran away and we've been looking for her for two years."

"Good line," said Huff. "Good line, but there's one little thing. You're white and she's black."

Roy looked at his arm as if he were seeing it for the first time.

"Duda's brown," shouted Scissors.

"Well, brown, black. Same difference," replied Huff.

"I can go," Pear offered with little enthusiasm. "I'm black."

"But they could have had a white father and a black mother," was Big Mouth's opinion. "It's anybody's guess what comes out."

"Duda's my foster sister," Roy decided. He got up. "Please, sir. My mother has been crying for three days straight already. I had

to get on four buses to come here. I spent the last of my money.
I just have to see her. Even if it's only for a minute."

Scissors applauded.

"Beautiful," said Huff. "I've got tears in my eyes already. You
could be an actor any day."

Roy went the next day. He returned at the end of the afternoon.
The boys were sitting together by the fountain. They jumped on
him when they saw him. "And? And?"

"I got there too late. She wasn't there anymore."

"You see? Duda's smart. She'll open all the doors." Alex nodded with satisfaction.

Big Mouth spread his arms wide as if he were holding up a
newspaper and read the pretend headline. "Breathtaking Escape
by Lady Thief."

"No," said Roy. "She got a job."

"A job?" the others cried in unison. "Duda a job?"

"Yeah," said Roy. "She got adopted. Or kind of adopted."

Adopted? Alex's heart soared, but then he grew cold inside.

Sitting on the rim of the fountain Roy recounted his adven-
tures and the boys listened breathlessly, because it was the kind
of story you only read in books.

The news story Scissors saw had been done right after Duda
was picked up, and it was about stealing and why a person steals.
Duda had talked about how she lived on the street, how she had
been caught and placed in juvenile detention. Then the reporter
had asked what she would like to be. She wanted to work with
children at a daycare center or as a receptionist in a big hotel,
she had said.

"What's that, a recessionist?" Scissors wanted to know.

"That's somebody at a hotel who gives you your key," said Roy.
"A lady with nylons and lipstick on."

Alex had to smirk. That's how Duda would put it. Duda, who always wore shorts, wearing nylons. In the heat and all. Her shoes would puddle up with sweat. Squish squish squish.

Roy went on. The daughter of a rich hotel owner had seen Duda. She had pestered her father until he had called the juvenile court judge. He wanted to offer Duda a job in one of his hotels. The judge had given the go-ahead.

"You mean the same one that wanted to get us off the street?" Huff wanted to know. "Then he's not so bad after all."

Roy didn't know. But he did know that Duda had it made. If she did her work well and didn't steal, then she could surely become a chambermaid. Then she'd be able to take an English course and, who knows, become a receptionist later on. That was what the doorman at Santos Dumont had told him.

"So what's she doing now?" asked Big Mouth.

"Uh, I don't know. Maybe she cleans," said Roy.

"We'll go find her. I want a job too," cried Scissors. "I can carry suitcases."

Roy acted as if he hadn't heard Scissors. "Duda was in the papers too."

"In the papers!" The Angels were all ears. The papers had carried a story about how Duda had been kept from going wrong and had been able to begin a new life, thanks to the girl and her rich father.

"Aw, that high-roller just wanted his fat face on the front page. That's why he helped Duda," said Huff.

"Where's the hotel?" Alex wanted to know. Maybe he could visit Duda.

Roy shook his head. "No idea. The doorman didn't know. He got it all from the paper. He only knew it was a big hotel somewhere in Copacabana."

"Copacabana?" the Angels cried in unison.

"That Duda sure got things set up good," Big Mouth concluded.

"But they said she lives somewhere else. In a house of some kind with other girls from the street. I think that's being paid for by Moneybags too," said Roy.

"I want Duda to come back," Pear said defiantly.

"Aw, man, she's never coming back. Co-pa-ca-ba-na … Hotel … Dollars …" Big Mouth said it as if he were a master of ceremonies.

"Are we going to look for Duda tomorrow?" Pear asked Roy.

"Where are we supposed to look? Pear, don't you worry. Sooner or later she'll be standing right here. I know for sure she's coming back. And I got friends in Copacabana and they know everybody and everything that's going on there. I'll get them on it."

"Hmmm, I bet they're those dopehead friends of yours," said Huff. "But when it comes to some huff, whoa, wait a minute."

Roy slugged him. His eyes were flashing. This meant a fight, thought Alex.

"Hey, boss," Huff sputtered. "Chill, man. I was joking."

Blackmail

As the noise gets less, the stench gets worse. Santa Luzia Street stank of urine, but you smelled it only at night. Alex was lying between Huff and Pear on a piece of cardboard. He held his mouth open a little and tried to breathe that way. Then you didn't smell as much, but your jaws got stiff.

He was thinking about Duda. "Who knows, maybe now you're lying in a bed with real sheets and you can smell the salt of the sea from Copacabana," he said softly. "You're listening to the waves breaking on the beach and to the music from a disco down on the street. Because of course you're living high up. Everything in Copacabana is high up and there are lots of discos. Maybe you'll even think about me, or about all of us, that's fine too. Then you'll be thinking of me a sixth of the time anyway."

Huff was snoring. Alex carefully rolled him onto his side.

Huff moved for a second and then went on sleeping. Pear was rolled up against Scissors. Big Mouth he could hardly see. He had hidden his head under his arms.

Now that he knew Duda wasn't living behind high walls anymore, Alex felt better. He had a mission: he was going to look for her. Tomorrow, early, he would ride to Copacabana on the bus and he would be sitting in front of a big hotel by seven o'clock. Because cleaners always came early. He would wait for her to come. And if she didn't come, he would sit in front of another big hotel the next day. He'd keep it up for as long as it took to find her.

He thought Roy was weird. Why didn't he go look for her? Didn't he miss her? Maybe he had another girlfriend. Why else would he be gone so much?

His left leg was asleep and he had to pee. Carefully he inched his bottom forward on the loose piece of cardboard in the direction of the wall. If he put his foot down straight he could push himself up on the wall. Then the blood would automatically run back into his leg. But the more strength he used, the more he slid down. The stoop was smooth and it slanted down. There was nothing special-looking about his sleeping leg. It was just as filthy as the other one. With two hands he grabbed the sleeping clump of flesh and poked it on the ground. Last night they had made it to the soup bus. That was why he had to go now—he had drunk two bowls of soup. His leg was starting to tingle. Slowly Alex got up. He chose a pillar on the other side of Santa Luzia Street for peeing.

When he got back, Huff had rolled onto his back again and had resumed snoring. Alex rolled him back and carefully lay down against him.

A bum was walking on the asphalt. He was pushing a hand-made cart loaded with a stack of cardboard. He must be hunting for a place to sleep. The wheels rattled like dry peas in a bus. The sound died down only long after he had rounded the corner.

Looking past the wheel of a parked car Alex saw a police cruiser coming. It was driving slowly. Because the windows were rolled down Alex could see that there were four of them inside. Should he wake Roy? But the car drove on.

He fantasized how it would be when he saw Duda. She would be surprised. He would say something smooth the way they do on television. My heart follows you always. No, that was too goopy. It had to be funny so she would laugh. He had found a bottle in the bay with a note with the address on it, he would tell her. The note had said ... Another car was driving down the street. Alex lowered his head behind his arm so he could spy without being seen. From behind the wheel of the parked car came a police cruiser. It was the same one. It was driving very slowly, just like before. When it had reached the corner, it stopped. Alex heard a dull click; with a whining engine the cruiser backed up fast. It stopped in front of the parked car, right near where they were lying. The doors opened. Alex's heart skipped a beat and his legs felt like mush.

"Roy, Roy." It was as if the hoarse shout that broke the silence of the night wasn't coming out of his own throat. Big Mouth and Roy bolted upright. Ready to jump on their attackers like crazed dogs, with pieces of glass and the knife.

Two officers had drawn their weapons. They wore gray police uniforms and had stocking caps on with only a slit for the eyes, so you couldn't see their faces. In the light of the arcade the handcuffs hanging from their belts glittered. There were two other officers sitting in the car.

"Stand up, scum. Out of here. This is not a place to sleep."

Pear, who was standing beside Alex, was shaking all over. Scissors started to cry softly. "Come on, stand up." An officer poked his foot into Scissors' emaciated body. Sobbing, Scissors looked for his blanket. "Leave that. You won't be needing that anymore," the officer snapped.

He wouldn't be needing his blanket anymore? Alex turned hot and cold at the same time, thinking that they'd had it— the cops were going to kill them for sure. They had to get away. He looked at Roy, but he didn't make a single sign. His eyes were empty, as if he didn't see.

"Sons of bitches," growled Huff.

"Something wrong?" The butt of the pistol landed squarely on Huff's temple. Huff staggered. Alex was able to grab him just in time. A trickle of blood was running down from under his hair.

"Start walking, bums." The officer nodded in the direction of the consulate.

They trudged one behind the other, Roy in the lead. Huff was holding his bruised temple with one of his hands. Pear was looking at the ground. Out of the corner of his eye Alex saw that the cruiser with the other two officers was keeping pace with them alongside the curb.

The street was desolate. At the consulate there was another police cruiser, but no people. Besides maybe the drunk, lying under the awning of a restaurant wrapped in newspaper. Now and then a car drove by, but nobody looked.

"Hurry it up a little." The barrel of a pistol poked Alex in the ribs. They crossed a street lined with trees. Even though it was dark, Alex knew where they were. During the day there were cars parked here. Were the cops bringing them to the park? Then they crossed an overpass; under it lived homeless families. They could get help. But deep in his heart Alex knew that they could do nothing and would do nothing. They would turn their backs and pretend they were asleep. People who snitch on murderers are themselves slated to die. They crossed a grassy area. The cruiser had disappeared. Now it was six to two. If they jumped them, all at the same time, they would have a chance. But how was he supposed to give the others a sign if they were walking single file? Now and then he saw the lights of a car racing through the park on the asphalt road.

He had to pray. God and his mother: they were the only ones who could help. Please, God, do something. Mama, help us. Right by the museum at the back of the park, they came to a halt. They were standing next to a parking lot under the trees. The squad car drove up slowly. It had gone around, of course, because it couldn't cross the grass.

"Hands on your heads," bellowed one of the two officers.

Scissors started to cry again.

"It's too late to feel sorry, you little delinquent," said the officer who Alex guessed was in command. "Robbing old ladies at knifepoint, you don't have any problem with that."

"But I don't have no knife," sobbed Scissors.

"Shut up."

"He's only ten," Pear said softly.

"That gal has something to say too," one of the officers said to the other. "Shut up, fag. A felon's a felon. Whether he's ten, fourteen, or forty."

Alex heard the click of a pistol safety. "You already walked around on this planet long enough."

"Noooooo!" Scissors' scream cut right to the quick.

"No?" said the officer. "I guess you mean yes. But first we're going to have us a little fun." He put the safety back on and gave Scissors a kick. After that he went over to Big Mouth and Roy.

Out of the corner of his eye Alex could see them falling to the ground.

"Stand up. Hands on your heads."

One of the officers from the car began to lay into Scissors with his nightstick. Scissors screamed, "Noooo, noooo!"

Alex felt rage boiling up inside. He wanted to grab the brute by the throat, but he knew it would be the stupidest thing he could do. He would be slaughtered like an animal. His arms were starting to feel heavy. He could hardly hold them up anymore.

Scissors was lying on the ground. The officer took a step to the side and headed for Alex.

Oh no, thought Alex. Automatically he lowered his arms in front of his face. The stick first hit him in the side. Then in the back. In the neck. He felt it everywhere. It burned. "You, free-loader," shouted the officer. Again the cudgel came down. "You're good for nothing." He wanted to scream, but no sound came. "Still have something to say before you die?" Alex raised his hand.

Suddenly it stopped. The truncheon wasn't coming down anymore.

"One-two, over to the wall." The officer kicked him in the ribs.

The six Angels were in a row facing the wall with their hands on their heads. Alex heard the safeties click. His legs were shaking. His whole body was limp. He couldn't think anymore. There was a whirlwind raging in his head. Now he was going to die. Suddenly he thought of his mother in the casket. The way she had quietly lain there. Now he would fly to her. Alex prepared himself for the pain. Even injections scared him. I want to die right away, he thought. He heard a dry crackle. It seemed like fireworks. And another one. And another one. It kept on crackling, exploding.

"I believe there's still one alive," he heard somebody say. He didn't dare look to the side at the others. My God, why hadn't they shot him? Why was he still standing here?

"OK, turn around, all of you," shouted somebody.

Alex jumped. All of you? Carefully he peered sideways as he

was turning around. There stood Pear. Scissors. Everybody was still alive. He didn't get it. What had happened? Down his leg ran something wet. His shorts were wet too. He had peed in his pants from fear. But what did that matter? They were alive.

The officers had removed their stocking caps. Two Alex recognized: they worked in the box on the square.

"That's the way we deal with felons," said the officer who seemed to be in charge. "But our friends can always count on our help." He looked from one face to the next. "We know you're felons, but we can get to be friends. You all jack. We get half. If you get caught, we'll make sure they let you go."

Alex looked sideways at the others, but it was dark out so he couldn't see their faces very well.

"The best thing is if you jack stuff on the square. Then we'll have everything under control."

The officer fell silent. The only sound was that of the insects buzzing in the lamp.

"Now I'd like to know which one of you freeloaders is going to accept our proposal," the officer continued. "Who wants to be our friend?" He let out a false laugh.

Nobody said anything. How do we get out of here? Alex was thinking. The officers were standing in a little cluster. If the Angels wanted to get away, they had to go over the grassy hill. The car couldn't go there.

It was as if Roy had read his thoughts.

"And?" the leader asked again.

"Nobody's going to be your friend," cried Roy. "Out of here, boys." He grabbed Scissors by the arm.

Alex turned around and ran. If only they didn't shoot. The grassy hill, the grassy hill, if only he reached it. He heard panting behind him and voices. The engine of the car started up. His leg hurt, but he forgot about it. He flew toward the hill.

Survivors

Saved. He was alive. That was the first thing he thought when he had crossed over the top of the hill. They hadn't shot and he was safe. He stood still beside a tree. His leg was burning. There was a stabbing pain in his side and he could hardly breathe. He had to grab hold of the tree trunk so he wouldn't collapse. He was exhausted. Those sons of bitches, killers, child beaters! He hated them.

In the semidarkness a shadow moved. Two, really. They weren't officers because their legs were bare and there were no shiny handcuffs.

"Yo," he whispered.

"Crusoe, it's us." He heard the panting voice of Big Mouth. "Pear and me."

"Man, we … have to … get out of here," said Alex, trying to

catch his breath.

"If you ask me, they got back in the cruiser. But then again, maybe not," said Big Mouth.

"If they were coming after us, they'd be here already," said Alex. "Where are Roy, Huff, and Scissors?"

"Don't know."

"They didn't get caught, did they?"

They stood there for another couple of minutes, hoping that the others would appear in the darkness. But nothing happened. Far away a car was honking, but other than that it was silent.

"We got to get out of here," said Big Mouth.

"Let's go to the rocks," Alex suggested. "We'll be safe there." He told Big Mouth and Pear about the pier and his secret spot. "But we have to take the back way because there are lots of lights along the footpath." The others agreed.

Alex led the way; he knew all the paths, hills, and bridges. They had been walking in silence for five minutes across the grass and under the trees when Alex heard something. He stood still. The leaves of the palm trees tapped in the wind like fine rain on a sheet-metal roof. The whispering started up again. It could be anything, thought Alex. Beggars, a couple having sex, or ...

"Pssstt," he said.

Pear pinched him in the arm. The whispering stopped, but nothing happened.

"Pssttt," Alex said again. "Roy?"

The branches rustled. Something snapped and then a man stepped out of the bushes. Alex squinted.

"That was a scare, man," said Roy.

"Roy." Pear threw himself into Roy's arms.

"Boy, *cara*, that you're here! We were scared ..."

"Crusoe." Scissors came limping out of the bushes and stuck

out both his arms. He almost shouted in his excitement.

"Ssttt," said Big Mouth. "You want to be beat to a pulp again?"

Alex grabbed Scissors under his armpits and held him close. He kissed his neck. And a few more times. He had never done that, but he was so happy that the boy was still standing in front of him alive and well.

"Where were you going?" asked Roy.

Again Alex explained in a whisper about the pier. Then in single file they sneaked through the dark park to the pier.

He wasn't sick but almost dead. That was what Alex thought when he woke up. The sun was shining in his face. All his joints hurt. He wanted to raise himself with his right arm, but he had no strength. It was as if he no longer had control over his own body. It looked different, too. In a single night he had turned into a zebra: he had welts all over.

His T-shirt was wet from the water in a little hollow in the rock he had half lain in during the night. His pants were sticky. With a lot of difficulty Alex took off his clothes. Then carefully he let himself slip off the stones and down into the water. The salt stung in the cuts, but in the cold water he slowly came back to life.

By the time he was back on the rocks, the others had woken up. Scissors had a hurt foot and, like Roy, had cuts all over from the bushes. Big Mouth had a shiner that was blue and puffed shut. Only Pear seemed to have gotten away from the encounter unharmed. If the memory of the previous night hadn't been so awful, Alex would have laughed at the sight of them all. The Lameduck Family Goes to the Beach.

"Let's go," said Roy.

"Go? Where to?" Big Mouth wanted to know. "I'm not going to the square anymore. I'm not crazy. That's where those brutes'll be."

Alex sided with him.

"Hey, where's Huff?" asked Scissors.

The others looked at one another. Huff! Nobody had thought about Huff. Had he run in a different direction last night? Had they caught him? Where was Huff?

"I'm going to ask around," said Alex. "I've got some acquaintances here. If a boy was killed in the park they'd know first thing." There was a sour taste in his mouth when he said "a boy." It was as if he were talking about somebody he didn't know. And that was true. The Huff he knew couldn't die; nobody could get Huff.

Luís, the utility shed guard, knew of nothing. He stared at the welts on Alex's arm but kept his mouth shut. Alex didn't say anything either. He didn't know if Luís would believe him, and he didn't feel like talking about his life on the street with glue sniffers either.

To make sure nothing had happened to Huff, he walked all the way to the museum. If Huff had been caught, he might still be lying there or there might be traces of blood. In the toll booth at the parking lot a man in coveralls sat reading the paper. The trees on the hilly green were in bloom. Greasy white flowers lay like carnival throws in the grass. Children were crowding around a popcorn cart in front of the museum entrance. Without his zebra arms Alex would have thought he had had a bad dream. Who could imagine that here, last night, six boys had almost been shot to death?

The others were relieved when he reported back. Huff had gotten away and he would turn up again somehow. That was the way things always went.

"We're going to Lapa," Roy announced.

It wasn't a good place to beg or steal, because it was where lots of poor people lived and there weren't any office buildings. But they couldn't go back to the square or to Santa Luzia Street. Roy knew about a nice spot to sleep in Lapa right near the

Arches. "The police don't go there," he said.

Everybody who lived on the street knew you had to watch out for the police. There were all kinds: thieves, rapists, abductors, and killers. Having rejected their offer, the Angels now knew something they weren't supposed to know. With it they had become dangerous to the officers. They could go to the papers or to the street children's organizations. As long as they were alive they could rat on the officers. And that meant they had called a death sentence down on themselves.

The spot Roy had thought of to sleep at was on a stairway, or rather on the landing of some stairs. The stairs were in a street with old houses, rooming houses, and little stores, leading up to a neighborhood on the top of a hill. After every fifty steps there was a level place where you could rest for a moment. That was where the Angels bedded down.

"A five-o can't get up here," Roy had said. "And if they come running up, we run up. And if they're standing at the top, we'll fly down."

"And if they're standing at the top and at the bottom?" Big Mouth had asked.

"You always have to be a wiseass?" Roy had said. He had walked away angrily. Roy wasn't himself, Alex felt. He was quick to anger, ate very little, and said hardly anything anymore. He must be sad. He had believed that the street belonged to everybody, and now he had seen that it wasn't so. He had been thrown out of his house, because for him Santa Luzia Street had been his house. Alex knew well what that felt like, being kicked out of your own house.

Big Mouth walked around cursing a blue streak. "You all frigging well better know that I plan on dancing Friday night. Police or no police."

Scissors was sad because now he couldn't watch any television. There weren't any electronics stores in Lapa. "We'll just have to go look around here in another neighborhood for a store," said Pear, trying to cheer him up.

"In Uruguaiana Street there was a jumbo screen," said Scissors. He brightened up only when Roy sent him on an important errand. He had to go to the square to see if Huff was hanging around anywhere. He was going to be a spy, as it were, on enemy territory, said Roy. Scissors jumped into his role in no time. The stick he'd found in the street became a spear with which he would fatally wound the enemy. He sneaked along the houses and peered all around. Until, as he was walking backward, he bumped into a woman coming out of a little grocery store.

She screamed and Scissors ran up the stairs. He was shaking all over. It took an hour for Roy to calm him down.

Scissors didn't see Huff on the square. He was still missing.

For sure he had gone to see his dope-dealing friends, thought Alex. He had said he would. He was sitting at the top of the hill with his gun. He was living well, shooting down anybody who tried to get him. Alex didn't know if he should envy him or not. Alex didn't know anything anymore. It was as if he had no feeling. The officers hadn't shot him, but they had gotten to him. Inside. If they had killed him, nobody would have known who he was. Nobody would have claimed his body. He was a nobody and he had nobody. He was sure nobody was going to adopt him. There were so many other, nicer-looking, better children without parents. What sense did it make to live anymore? He might as well be dead.

That he was going to look for Duda in Copacabana wasn't important anymore. In fact, he no longer really believed in it. If he found her, she wouldn't go with him anyway. Maybe she would pretend she didn't know him. Now she had a job and a house. She was fancy.

Alex couldn't sleep at night, so he stared at the sky a lot. Was his mother looking at him from behind that blanket of stars? Maybe she had something against him now.

The stairway was lit up but it was quiet on the street. It made Alex scared. One night somebody had tossed buckets of water down the steps. At first they hadn't noticed anything, but when it started pouring down it was too late. Their clothes were wet. For once they moved down to the sidewalk below.

They went to the bathroom near the Arches. There was an area where people threw garbage bags and parked their cars. You could get water at the gas station. Alex washed his clothes in the bay. Roy had found a valet who was willing to buy them a can of glue for a fat fee.

For begging and stealing the pickings were very scant in their new street, especially during the week if there weren't any bands playing. Then there wasn't much "movement," as the boys called it.

One evening Big Mouth scored fifteen *real* and a watch. He had jumped an old man coming out of the little grocery store under the Arches. The man had handed everything over right away.

Big Mouth's joy over the fifteen *real* disappeared when Pencil, the hustler at the Central Station, would give him only five *real* for the watch. "Bastard. Even treats a kid like shit!" Big Mouth complained to everybody who would listen.

Another day Alex, Pear, and Big Mouth surrounded a woman who was waiting for the bus. But she had such a set of lungs that everybody stared and they had to run away fast so as not to get caught.

Resistance in the neighborhood was growing. "They should deport you all," the woman from the poultry shop would shout whenever they passed by. One evening a broad-shouldered bruiser walked over to Roy. "If you all don't behave, you know what's going to happen," he said.

Roy decided they had to leave. Maybe it was a good idea to be out of Rio entirely for a time. He had an aunt with a farm in Minas Gerais province. There was enough room there for everybody. Nobody said anything.

"Don't you think it's a good idea?" asked Roy.

"Yeeaahh," said Pear. "But I've never traveled anywhere before."

"How many buses we got to take?" Big Mouth wanted to know.

"One," said Roy. "But it takes a day and a half for it to get there."

"Are there animals on the farm?" asked Scissors.

What a stupid question, thought Alex. "You ever seen a farm without any animals?"

"But what is it? A farm?" asked Scissors.

Everybody felt like going on a trip. Now, the money. They needed money for the bus and they couldn't all show up at the aunt's empty-handed.

"We have to think of something. Or else we'll still be sitting here next week," said Roy.

"Let's kidnap somebody," said Big Mouth. "Every week somebody gets kidnapped and you ever seen what they ask? Sometimes a million!"

"We're going to rob a bank," cried Scissors. "Boo-ya, boo-ya, boo-ya. Dead."

But all that was bunk. Nobody had a really good idea.

One of the many times Alex woke up that night, he looked around and Roy was gone.

The Trap

Roy stayed away. It was close to noon by the time he came back. The Angels had taken the little tram back and forth twice and were lying under the Arches kicked back on an old mattress they had found.

Something was up, Alex could tell right away. Roy was nervous and had a plastic bag with him.

He motioned the others over. They squatted behind a parked car. Roy opened the bag.

"Damn, a thirty-eight." Big Mouth was all admiration. Alex was shocked. It was no joke. Roy was holding a gun in his hand. Alex didn't know the difference between a revolver and a pistol, but it looked real. It was black and there was a chamber with little holes for the bullets.

"Look," said Roy and he reached into the bag again.

"Another one?" asked Pear. There was a second gun lying on the ground, a little smaller but almost the same. Out of his pockets Roy pulled little metal slugs. "Bullets," he said and sprinkled them on the plastic bag as if they were confetti.

Scissors grabbed for them. "They look like little bombs."

Alex shuddered. If one of those slugs entered your body, straight through your skin, you were dead.

How had Roy come by the guns?

"Borrowed," said Roy.

"Borrowed?" repeated Big Mouth. "Borrowed from who? Not from our friends the police officers?"

"No, I got contacts," Roy said mysteriously. "We rented them for twenty-four hours. Tomorrow night the stuff has to be back. If not, then …" He drew a straight line in the air with his forefinger. That was street talk. Alex was familiar with the gesture; it meant "kill, shoot dead."

"Hey, look." Big Mouth was striding around the cars, the revolver stuck in his waistband, wooden butt-end up. Suddenly he jumped into a wide-legged stance, grabbed the gun, and aimed with arms straight out at an imaginary enemy. "Stand still, you. Stand or I'll shoot."

"Rambo, Rambo." Scissors was jumping up and down wildly. "My turn. My turn. Give me."

"Stop dumbing, man. You're not a kid anymore," Roy said angrily to Big Mouth. He got up and pulled the gun out of his hands. "In a minute they'll see us." Roy put everything back in the plastic bag.

"What are we going to do with those guns?" asked Alex, motioning toward the bag.

"Rob a bank," said Big Mouth.

Roy shook his head. "That won't work. You want to die? Two guns is way too few for a bank robbery. Every bank has at least two guards, *cara*."

"Why don't we go stand at the stoplights?" asked Pear. "If they see you with a gun they'll hand over everything. Jackpot."

Big Mouth protested vehemently. "Aw, no. What you got then? You'll be sitting there with five watches and then that bastard at the Central'll give you five *real* for them."

"I thought we could hold up a bus," said Roy. "One that's full. Then we'll be hitting lots of birds with one stone."

Big Mouth clicked his tongue. "Totally dope, boss. I'm with you." Pear and Scissors were enthusiastic too.

"And you, Crusoe. Why're you not saying anything?"

Alex started. He felt as if he were slowly sliding into a deep, dark hole. There was nothing to hang on to on the slippery slope. They would laugh at him if he said he was scared. They might think he was going to squeal on them. Maybe they would kill him. They had guns now, after all. He had never really been one of them. So why not. He sighed and thought of Duda in her other life. She had been right not to come back. One day she would walk around in nylons and have a house with a bathroom. Because she was different. She was pretty and she was a woman.

"Well, Crusoe. What are you sighing about?"

Alex nodded. "I'm in."

"Fine. That's what I like to hear," said Roy.

And he explained the way he had thought it out. They would take line 174. It was always full and drove through Flamengo Park. They could get away there easily after they had robbed the passengers.

He and Big Mouth would buy tickets and walk to the front. They would have the guns hidden under their clothes. Alex and Pear would get on at the next stop so as not to create suspicion and would stand in the back. They would have plastic bags with them in which to put the money, jewelry, and watches.

Roy was to give the signal. He would shout: This is a holdup. Hands up. After that Pear and Alex would walk down the aisle with their plastic bags.

"But what if there are soldiers on the bus?" asked Big Mouth.

"Yeah, well then we won't do anything, of course," said Roy. "We can't have any shooting. Soldiers, police. Men with loose shirts are dangerous too. They often carry a gun under there."

Big Mouth nodded. Alex caught himself wanting to run away. But where to?

"What about me? What do I do?" asked Scissors.

"You, Scissors, you have to guard the house."

"The house?" said Scissors.

"Joke, man. You're staying here. You're too little."

Scissors fixed Roy with a stare. When it dawned on him that Roy was serious, he jumped on him. "I want to go too. I'm going too." With both fists he thumped Roy's chest.

Roy grabbed him by the arm, slammed him up against a car, and shoved his knee into Scissors' stomach.

"You don't have any want-to's. Understood? We can't use you on the bus. This is something different from making life difficult for little old ladies." Scissors said nothing and Roy let him go.

Alex saw Big Mouth right away when the bus stopped. He was sitting in the first seat next to the window, beside an old woman. He showed no sign of recognition. Alex discovered Roy only after he had gotten on. Roy was standing in the aisle, checking out all the passengers. There was one seat left in the back of the bus next to two girls in school uniforms. They held their knapsacks in their laps. An old black man with white hair was looking out the window. A fat lady wearing a flowered dress was talking to her little boy, who was sitting on her lap. He was sure she was from the northeast, judging by her face. The two in front of her must be two gringos. You could tell right off. White legs and wearing those weird shoes. They could be the first ones to hand over their goodies when the time came. The fat man with the pink shirt on, on the other side. Was that shirt hanging loose or was it tucked into the pants? He had to pay attention to that, Roy had said. But from the back of the bus you couldn't tell at all which way the shirt was.

Roy winked at him. Alex jumped. Now it was going to happen. His heart pounded and his mouth felt dry.

"This is a holdup. Anybody moves and I shoot them dead. Hands on your heads, all of you." Roy waved the gun around.

With a jolt the bus came to a stop. "Help, a holdup. A holdup. Police." One woman was hanging out the window and was yelling at passersby.

"Shut up," roared Roy.

Alex was shaking all over. He gripped the metal handle above his head. He had the feeling that he couldn't breathe. He could still turn back. If he didn't do anything, nobody would know that he was part of it. The police might get there in two seconds, if anybody had heard the woman. As long as Roy didn't look at him.

What about Pear?

He heard nothing behind him that sounded like money being collected and watches being snatched.

"Hands up," shouted Roy. "Everybody. Or else I'll shoot them off."

There was an explosion followed by tinkling. There was a hole with a star in the windshield. Who had shot? People screamed. There were flashes and more explosions. Alex felt people pushing and the next minute he was lying on the floor, crushed between clawing people trying to get to the exit. Big Mouth was crouched beside the driver's seat eyeing every direction, his revolver at the ready.

"Help, help," somebody yelled. Children were crying. In the aisle people lay on top of each other; others were hiding behind the seats. On the back of a seat a gun barrel appeared. Out of the barrel came a flash and after that a little puff of smoke. Big Mouth ducked out of sight.

Where was Roy? thought Alex. Suddenly he caught sight of him. He had been lying between two seats and was standing in the aisle. His face was sweaty and he had a scratch on his left cheek. He jumped up on a seat and dove for a window. God, was he going to climb out of the window?

Another gunshot sounded and more tinkling. On hands and knees Alex tried to get to the aisle to see what had happened. He was still able to glimpse Roy's two wildly kicking legs disappear out the window. He heard a thud. He was sure Roy had fallen down. Big Mouth had disappeared. Pear seemed to have been swallowed up by the ground.

And he? He was crawling around like some kind of idiot. In a minute he'd be caught. Alex counted to three, took a deep breath, and then jumped over the exit step and outside.

When he felt the asphalt under his feet, he started running. First he ran down the street and then he took to the sidewalk, jumping over the holes and zigzagging around the people. Only when he had reached Gloria Square did he slow down. Where were his flip-flops? He had probably lost them in the battle on the bus. He hadn't even noticed he'd been running barefoot.

At a cement table under the trees he stopped to rest. After a half hour he slowly walked back. The bus was still parked slanted across the road in the place he had left it. Curious onlookers crowded around. Alex squeezed between the people until he was in the front row. He was shocked.

On the asphalt lay Roy. His legs were spread apart. His pants were ripped and beyond that he was unrecognizable. His head lay in a big pool of blood. It was crushed. There weren't any eyes or nose anymore, only a big gaping hole, blood, hair, and something that looked like skin. Revolted, Alex looked away. He felt light-headed and his stomach was turning.

"An armed robber. Had a revolver and everything," a man behind him said. Alex pricked up his ears. "They wanted to grab him, but then he jumped out the window. They say the other bus ran him over on purpose. He was driving behind and of course saw everything. No fun being a bus driver these days with all those holdups. Those guys are violent."

"You said it. The only good thief is a dead thief. If you hand them over to the police, they're out on the streets again tomorrow. They're a plague."

It wasn't true. Alex didn't want to believe it. Run over. Crushed like a cockroach under the heel of a shoe. He turned around wildly and elbowed his way back out through the crowd of people. "Behave yourself a little," a man shouted.

"Bastard," said Alex.

He walked without knowing where he was going. A fog hung before his eyes and his legs moved automatically. Alex bumped into a trash can, but he didn't feel it. Now they wouldn't be taking any trips, thought Alex.

A man in a shiny shirt was headed toward him. His face was big and red and he was careening over the sidewalk as if he were dribbling around half a dozen opponents on a soccer field. Then he stood still in front of Alex. He had trouble keeping his balance, first on one leg, then on the other. He stared at Alex.

"Good work. Now you, loafer."

"Say that again, bastard." Alex had grabbed a piece of wood off the street and was swinging it. "I'll smash your brains in."

"Hey, hey, easy there," cried a passerby.

Robinson Crusoe

Night had fallen. Alex was sitting on the grass near the airport. How he had gotten there and what he was doing next, he didn't know. He had walked like a blindfolded cow. His ears hurt from the airplane that had just shrieked to a landing. It was taxiing over the concrete squares toward the lit-up building.

He had to get out of here. But where to? Suddenly Alex felt a fear he had never felt before. Maybe he would be recognized on the street as one of the holdup men. He was sure they would have noticed that he was with Roy and Big Mouth.

And the guns. He had forgotten about them. They had to be delivered tonight. He couldn't under any circumstances go back to the stairs in Lapa. Roy's friends might be standing there waiting. Would they shoot and kill him if he told them the Angels had lost the guns?

The wind brought him snatches of music. In front of a trailer rigged up as a bar along the road a couple was kissing. A fat woman in shorts came down the steps. She was carrying a tray with two bottles on it.

Suddenly he knew: he would go to the beach. Maybe Dona Lica was still there. If she wasn't there anymore, he would go to her house. Dona Lica would help him.

But Dona Lica wasn't there. The two Styrofoam coolers in which she kept bottles chilled during the day, the beach parasols, and the folding chairs had been hidden under a plastic tarp. In the sand lay a boy holding a little radio to his ear. He had to keep an eye on things for Dona Lica until the next morning, he said. Where Dona Lica lived he didn't know. Then he put the radio up to his ear again, looking at Alex's bare feet and the scars on his legs. He knew but he wasn't telling, thought Alex, because he was from the street. Angry, Alex turned around. He drank some water from the tap and bolted down a sausage roll he bought with the three *real* he still had on him. He was in a hurry. The world seemed to be filled with enemies. Before the beach was empty he had to have a spot. Four walls that would protect him.

Luís, of course! Stupid that he hadn't thought of him earlier. He was sitting on a chair beside the fence.

"Can I sleep here tonight?" asked Alex.

Luís sighed.

"It's only for one night. I swear to God. After that I'm going to my aunt's house."

Luís squinted around and then leaned forward. "Come back after ten. Then the night crew's gone home. I don't want any problems."

At quarter past ten Alex dragged himself to the shack. Luís was sitting in the same spot and was listening to a soccer match on the radio. He looked to see if there was anyone around and then slid the gate open. "Lie back behind there," he said and pointed at a pile of cement bags. "There are some empty bags there, you can spread them out on the ground. Early tomorrow morning, at six o'clock, you have to be out of here. At six-thirty the first of them'll be standing at the gate. Understood?"

Alex nodded. He was happy that Luís hadn't asked any questions. What was he supposed to say?

For the first time he was sleeping outside without having to worry about attackers. There were walls and Luís was sitting in the chair. Still, the night on the cement bags was one of the most miserable of all his nights on the street.

His thoughts churned at top speed. Where should he go tomorrow? Back to the trains? Back to Japeri where his stepfather wanted to shoot him? Back to the park? Why, he wondered. Why did he have to go anywhere? Why couldn't he just die?

It was a clear, balmy night. Alex looked up. He missed her. She was so far away. If only she could come down for a little while. A day's outing. Half an hour was all right too. He knew that it was childish. She wouldn't come. Well, he would go see her. She was upset. He could feel she was upset. But I don't want this life anymore, he said, hoping she wanted to listen. There's no use in it. I'm dead tired. I don't want to fight anymore. Why should I? They'll shoot me anyway. Or they'll run me down.

She said nothing. He waited; maybe she was thinking it over. But she still didn't say anything. So he started talking again. I really want death over this life. I want to be with you. Don't you like the idea of me coming to see you?

She kept her silence; was she angry?

He reflected. Strange: suddenly he knew what he wanted. He wanted to stop. Dying wasn't bad as long as it didn't hurt. He had figured it out: he would walk into the ocean. He would lie on his back in the waves and look at the sun. The ocean would rock him to and fro and then he would go under forever. It wouldn't work in the bay. That wasn't really the ocean. All the way to the end of Copacabana, there was a rock jutting out into the ocean, with high waves all around it. That was where he would go. He would let himself slip into the water from the rocks. A beautiful death in a beautiful place. The plan didn't make Alex sad. No, he was relieved.

He opened his eyes wide. Don't be angry. I'm coming.

At five-thirty Luís woke him up. "Be quick, boy. In a minute the morning crew'll be here."

Half asleep, Alex stumbled out. Above the bay the sun was coming up like a fiery ball. The first of the joggers were running along the footpath.

"Go lie down on the cement bench in front here. I'll keep an eye out," Luís called as he slid the gate shut.

Alex lay down. He was so exhausted that he fell asleep again right away. At eight o'clock he woke up with a jolt. The sun was burning on his face, his mouth was dry, and he had to pee badly. At the end of the bench there was an elderly white man wearing shorts. With both hands he was leaning on a cane in front of him. Now and then it wobbled, along with his head. People wearing sun visors strolled along the footpath on the beach. Alex heard a bicycle bell.

He had to get going. Today he had important business to do. He looked for his flip-flops. Suddenly he remembered that he had lost them on the bus. He saw himself crawling on the floor and Roy's legs disappearing out the window.

But he didn't want to think about that anymore. If it happened again, he'd count to a hundred, he decided.

He walked across the rolling green to Gloria Square. At a

bakery he bought coffee and a buttered roll. This would be his last coffee and his last roll. When he had finished, he would catch the bus to Copacabana.

A beer delivery man knocked back a cognac and stared at his bare legs.

"Go look at yourself," said Alex.

He went over to stand beside a girl drinking a soda. She immediately moved over and snatched her purse away.

He waved his ticket, but the man on the other side of the counter acted as if he'd seen nothing. He looked the other way every time. Only when Alex slammed his open palm on the glass case did he hurry over.

"Going to smash it? Go right ahead, as long as you know I'll smash your head in first," the man yelled.

Suddenly Alex saw Roy's face without a nose. He bolted down the roll. He had to get out of here.

When he walked out of the bakery, it happened. On the side of a kiosk he saw it. Roy's face without a nose was there, as big as life, on the front page of a newspaper. The elephant T-shirt in a pool of blood. "Robber Run Over," the headline said. And below that, "Crime Doesn't Pay." Alex started reading:

> A robber attempting to hold up bus 174 yesterday afternoon was struck by a second bus while escaping. He died instantly. The identity of the man, Caucasian and presumably in his early twenties, has not been established. According to passengers who wish to remain anonymous, two robbers got on at the Tiradentes Square stop. When the bus reached Flamengo Park the two announced a holdup. An armed pas-

senger responded. A shootout followed. One of the holdup men attempted to escape through a window. According to eyewitnesses, he fell to the pavement. A bus driving behind was unable to avoid hitting him. The second robber, whom passengers described as a black youth, managed to get away.

"They sure got him," said a cabdriver as he pointed out the photograph to his colleague. "Look, his brains are even coming out."

Alex stood in front of the paper without moving, frozen. His heart felt cold. Then he shouted, "It's a lie. It's a lie. He drove over him on purpose."

The cabdrivers looked at each other and then shook their heads. But Alex didn't see. He had turned around and was walking to the bus stop. He moved slowly; his legs were heavy. The cars honked when he crossed. Alex heard nothing. He walked between the bumpers and looked neither left nor right.

It was all lies. Roy wasn't dead. He couldn't die, because Angels don't die. Roy was alive and he was bigger and stronger than ever. Alex closed his eyes and said softly, "Hey, boss. Boss, where are you? You hear me?"

The people at the bus stop stared at the strange boy talking to himself. The bus to Copacabana stopped along the curb, its brakes screeching, and the back door flipped open.

Then Alex saw him. He was carrying his flip-flops in his hand because he was running. "Roy, wait. Roy, wait for me," he yelled.

Roy turned around. He smiled and waved. "We're going over to the rocks. See you there," he shouted and rushed off.

Out of breath, Alex reached the pier. Sweat was running in rivulets down his back and into his shorts. Panting, he squinted along the pier with his hand over his eyes. He didn't see Roy. He must be at the point because he had to watch out for his pursuers. Roy was smart. Alex climbed up the rocks. He jumped from one block of stone to the next until he had reached the point. His heart was beating in his throat.

But where was Roy? He was going to be waiting for Alex here, wasn't he? He had said "the rocks," hadn't he?

Alex called. And a few more times, louder each time. "Roy ... Roy ... Roy?" There was only the sound of the water slapping on the rocks and the faraway murmur of voices on the beach. A seagull bobbed on a wave. The buildings on the other side of the bay looked as if they were made of silver because of the sun. Alex sat down. It couldn't be true. Roy wasn't there. The gull flapped away. A beetle ran across a block of stone and shot away into a crack. Alex's eyes were burning, and then he began to cry without a sound. More and more tears welled up. They drew wet stripes down his cheeks. The stripes became rivers and the rivers dripped on the rocks. It was like a tropical rainstorm after years of drought. All his sorrow spilled out. His body jerked, and now and then a high-pitched sigh escaped him.

Alex was crying so hard that he didn't hear somebody coming. Suddenly he felt a hand on his neck. "Hey, Crusoe, what's all this?" Alex whipped around and through his tears he was looking into Duda's face.

"Duda, Duda, he ..." But his voice faded away.

Duda blinked her eyes and pursed her lips. "Ssshhh. Crusoe, I saw it in the paper. The picture. I looked for you all morning. Then I came here. I was hoping you'd be here."

She sat down and pulled him against her. Alex didn't say anything. He couldn't. He cried with big sobs against Duda's breast and threw his arms around her waist. He lay that way for at least twenty minutes, as if he had been glued with Elmer's glue and couldn't get unstuck anymore.

"Nobody's going to break us, Crusoe," whispered Duda. She ran her fingers over his hair. "Together we're strong. They won't get us. You know that, don't you?"

He nodded his head. Of course he knew that.

There was a moment of silence. Then Alex took a deep breath. "Duda?" His voice sounded hoarse and hiccuped as if it weren't his anymore. "Duda, Robin … Robinson Crusoe … "

"What, Crusoe, what about Robinson Crusoe?"

"Did somebody come to rescue him or did he die?"

Duda frowned. "If you ask me, he was rescued. How else would we know his story? You sure ask weird questions. Let's go, because I'm starving. Think you can walk?"

Alex said nothing. He had turned around in Duda's lap and was looking out over the bay full of sailboats.

Afterword

Alex is real. Only his name is made up. Since March 1995, Alex has been living with fourteen other boys in the São Martinho homeless shelter in Rio de Janeiro. He has a day job in an office as their youngest clerk and goes to night school.

Exactly how many street children there are in Brazil, nobody knows. Counting is difficult in the first place because Brazil is incredibly big. It is the fifth-largest country in the world, only slightly smaller than the United States, and almost sixty million children and teenagers live there. And then there's the problem that the lives of people living on the street change rapidly. No sooner has everybody been counted than you can start all over again.

But there is another reason for the uncertainty. When are you a street child, really? Are children who sell candy during the day at the stoplights or who haul a shoeshine box around all day but sleep at home at night, street children? And what do you call kids who usually sleep at home but sometimes on the street? Some people believe that you can call any children who spend the greater part of the day on the street, street children. Others say no, a street child is a child who lives on the street day and night. This makes for great differences when you start counting, because there are hundreds of thousands of children in Brazil who work on the street but a lot fewer who spend every night there as well. The number is suspected to be no more than ten thousand.

A couple of years ago they took a head count in Rio. Researchers drove through the entire city for two nights at different times. They counted 837 children who were really sleeping on the street. That was a much smaller number than everybody had always thought.

They discovered that children almost never sleep alone. More than half, usually the littlest ones and the girls, live with their mother or parents on the street. The family can no longer pay the rent and has moved to the sidewalk.

What is happening more and more often is that the parents work but don't earn enough money to be able to go home on the bus every day. So the family will sleep on the street during the week and go home only on the weekend.

Many children sleep usually in groups and now and then by themselves. Girls never sleep alone at night. That's very dangerous. There are far fewer girls than boys on the streets anyway.

There are lots of reasons why children go live on the street. A large number of children in poor neighborhoods hang around outside most of the day. Because there are too many children for too few schools, children in Brazil go to school in shifts. You go to school either in the morning or in the afternoon—that is, if the school hasn't been shut down because of other problems.

This, among other reasons, is why more than half of the children don't finish elementary school. Those who do, end up staying behind three times on average. If there is no school or you can't go on to the next grade, the step to the street is small.

The most important reason why children go live on the street is poverty. It usually starts when there isn't enough to eat at home. By shining shoes, washing cars, parking cars, selling candy, and panhandling, children try to help their parents out. They are registered at a school but have no time to go.

Sometimes they steal a little if they can't manage to earn. Girls usually earn a little extra by sleeping with men.

In Rio de Janeiro it is very normal to run into a child somewhere at ten o'clock at night selling peanuts or roses who still has to ride the bus for an hour to get home. In order to have a little fun and sometimes to forget their hunger, almost all street children use drugs, especially glue.

They often think of suicide. In São Paulo, the biggest city in Brazil, researchers interviewed 150 street children two years ago. A quarter of them said that they had tried to commit suicide at least once.

During the past years there has been a lot of concern overseas about street children being murdered. But it is difficult to get figures even on this. There are murders that are never reported because people are scared. Sometimes the reports include children that are injured and die later on. The available figures concern children and teenagers in general. They don't mention how many of them live on the streets.

Recently a study was completed in the province of Rio de Janeiro. At least three teenagers or children are murdered there every day. All killings in a time period of three years were checked, as well as where the killings took place. It now appears that most killings are not of street children. Nor would the word "children" even be appropriate.

Who are the top scorers on the death charts? Boys of seventeen—so, almost adult—who live in ghettos. They are involved in the drug business and are shot in the ghettos (a fate presumably awaiting Huff). The older they are, the greater the chance that they will be shot and killed. Eighty percent—that's four out of five—of the young people who were killed on the street turned out to be fifteen or older. This number included few real children, those aged eleven years old and younger. Of these, fewer than one out of ten were victims.

The overwhelming majority of children who are killed are killed at home—by the father or mother, the stepfather, brother, or other family member. The mother tells the police that the child fell off the roof. At the hospital the doctor sees that the child was beaten to death. It is, by the way, not true that you don't have to be scared of your violent father or foster father when you are older. One in five killings in the older age group (twelve to seventeen) occurred at home. Alex might have ended up in this category if he had stayed at home.

What about police involvement? Researchers believe that the police have been the perpetrators in slightly more than ten percent of all killings.

When the police catch you stealing or doing even worse things, they take you down to the police station. There a report is written up. The juvenile court judge must decide within two days what is to happen in the short term. In Rio de Janeiro there is only one juvenile court judge who decides this.

You have to wait a month and a half for the actual trial. If the offender is younger than twelve, he or she will go for a couple of weeks to a place that has been OK'd by the juvenile court judge but has nothing to do with prison. If the offender is older but not yet eighteen, he will go to the Padre Severino detention center. That is an institution holding hundreds of boys who have stolen or even killed and who have not yet been sentenced. For girls there is another center called Santos Dumont.

The juvenile court judge can decide many things during the trial. Often he will send children back to their parents, or else he will seek out a foster family. He can have the older ones do community service work or sentence them to a prison term. There is a special juvenile prison for that.

It regularly happens that the police do not do their work well. They beat the boys up and then put them out on the street again. Or they catch young thieves and take them to the station and there, behind closed doors, make deals. If the boys deliver the goods, they don't have to go to the juvenile court judge.

Alex ended up in a homeless shelter for street children: São Martinho. São Martinho is a foundation in Rio de Janeiro that does a lot for street children. There is a cantina where street children can eat for free during the afternoon. There are homes and vocational courses. In addition, ex-street children are helped in finding jobs. There are many unemployed people in Brazil, and because street children have a bad reputation and tend not to have spent much time in school, it is even more difficult for them to find work.

Luckily there are more foundations and people who do good work for street children. In the city of Salvador, about a thousand miles north along the coast from Rio, ex-street children set up their own paper factory with the help of adults. The cities of São Paulo (some 250 miles down the coast from Rio) and Fortaleza (on the northern coast of Brazil) have circuses made up of street children.

Over the past decade a kind of union has been set up by and for street children, the National Movement of Street Children, in which street-corner workers and children across the entire country work together. Unfortunately there are also many organizations that claim they are doing something but that exist primarily to attract money from overseas.

And if a street child ends up in a homeless shelter, as Alex did, does everything turn out well? No, not automatically. That's where a new struggle takes place. Especially with yourself. You have to have a will of steel to be able to handle the new life.

Anybody used to the freedom of the streets doesn't really want to go home at nine o'clock just when a big party's starting. Every day and night you sniffed glue, and now drugs have suddenly been forbidden. If others steal your pants, you can't beat them up or steal something back. That's tough.

It is also difficult to get up every day at six o'clock to go to work, where you often earn a lot less than you did before, stealing on the street.

After many years you're back at school. You want to learn, but as you sit down on the school bench you discover you're one of the worst in the class.

You've got a kind of a house; you can't complain. But you always have to share everything with many others. Food, television, a room, an outing. Never is there anything for you and only you—a private place, or a dessert you like. Sometimes you really have a craving for that.

All in all, it's difficult to get used to quickly. Street children cannot often handle life in a shelter and return to the streets. This can go on for a time: being in a home, being on the street.

Ineke Holtwijk
Rio de Janeiro, June 1995

Glossary

Botafogo: a Rio de Janeiro soccer team.

Cachaçeiro: someone who drinks a lot of rum, cane sugar rum.

Cara: literally means "face." But on the street it is used in addressing people. Then it means "man," or "boy."

Copacabana: a district of Rio de Janeiro famous because it is located along a beautiful sandy beach. The name derives from an Indian language and means "view over the blue."

Exu: pronounced like A Shoe. Exu is an African god that is much like the devil of European beliefs. He can help you, but he is quick to anger. Then he'll do everything to break you. In Brazil lots of people believe in African gods. They make sacrifices to them because they believe that they will then receive help. The African gods came to Brazil with the slaves that were brought over from Africa and had to work on the sugarcane plantations.

Flamengo: a Rio de Janeiro soccer team. Flamengo is the team for which Romario plays now. Flamengo is also the name of a rich neighborhood.

Lapa: district in Rio de Janeiro very close to downtown.

Morro da Providencia: Mountain of Sustenance. It is the name of a ghetto in downtown Rio de Janeiro. Rio is a city with many hills and mountains. Because the hills are too steep to build houses or apartment buildings on, the poor used to build their little huts there in secret. Gradually these became entire ghetto areas.

Real: The monetary unit used in Brazil. A *real* is worth about one U.S. dollar. There are a hundred *centavos* in a *real.*

Samba stadium: Rio's famous carnival parades are held in a stadium that looks like a stretch of road with bleachers on either side.

Santos Dumont: name of the juvenile detention center for girls. Santos Dumont was a Brazilian who, according to the Brazilians, discovered flying.

São Martinho: a foundation in Rio de Janeiro with a cantina, a nurse, and courses and residences for street children.

Ineke Holtwijk is a correspondent in Latin America for leading Dutch newspapers and for the news on television for young people. She is based in Rio de Janeiro. Before she wrote this book, she spent a lot of time with a group of children who live in the streets. Alex, the main character of *Asphalt Angels*, is a real person and all the events in the book are based on real events.

Wanda Boeke is a professional translator who has worked with a variety of writers and filmmakers in the Netherlands, France, Belgium, and Spain. Her translations published in the Netherlands, Great Britain, and the United States, include contributions to *Cimarron Review, Exchanges, Dutch Crossing, Poetry International, the Greenfield Review,* and *Callaloo.* Recent publication of *Unnatural Mothers* and *The Cockatoo's Lie* introduced Dutch novelists Renate Dorrestein and Marion Bloem to American readers.